Squid People

By Randall Herrera

Copyright © 2018 Randall Herrera | **ISBN:** 9781723882999

Dedicated to Melanie, Jadyn, Reece and Cruz.
Weird people are the best people. Love Always.

Chapter 1 – Memories die hard

Small town Sheffield Iowa, a man nervously paces back and forth in a room. As he chews his nails he looks onto a frail aging women sitting on the edge of a bed. You can tell he's concerned about her well-being, these could be the last days of her life. The staff are nice but you can see it in their eyes that we're in our final stages of farewells. A breeze gently blows through the open window, you can hear the small whistle it makes as it pushes back and forth on the screen. "Mom" he says. She doesn't react. Her mind is gone and her eyes dart back and forth with lost thoughts of the farm and her 54 years of marriage. "Mom" he politely requests again, but this time moving closer to her bed. She blinks her eyes and looks towards the room door as if she's heard him but can't yet form the words. "Mom, we need to figure out what you want to do with farm? I have a gentlemen here that can help..." The woman interrupts with exasperated "ENOUGH... nuff. 35 years Henry. 35 years old and you still can't even tie your own shoes. Let alone make any sort of a reasonable decision. Look at who you married." "Mom," Henry quickly interjects before the conversation heads down a familiar road. "Mother, these are things that are in your name and I have no authority to even..."

"To even what Henry?" She now looks at him directly in the eyes. "Before you can drain every last cent out of your father and me?" The woman struggles to pull her blankets up over her legs as she continues. "You know, you're father's last words on this earth were all about you. Not the good times, dreams we had or could have's, but about you and your future. What have you got Henry? What have you done to make him proud besides add to his debt?

Henry calmly replies, "Mom, I've done everything I could for you and dad and I appreciate all that you have done. I've tried." Henry's voice cracks a bit, "I've stayed in this shit town for all of these years just to be sure someone would be here, like now, in these times. Like I was there when dad died."

"YOU WERE THERE to see how much he left you.. period. Henry has always been about Henry. I'm actually shocked that your wife could see something in you that I never could."

The woman stops, almost in mid-sentence, and returns to looking out the window.

Henry now stands there with the realization of just how much disdain his mother has held for him all of these years. He wonders to himself is it the dementia that's bringing on this unneeded cruelty? Or are these her true feelings? In the last few days in anyone's life I'm sure people say things that they don't mean or even things that are completely false. But this, this seemed like it's been a burden she's been holding onto for years. So many years that it's engrained into who she's now become.

   Just then the door slowly opens to the room and a little girl's face appears from behind the door. She doesn't fully enter the room only because she has been told numerous times that grandma isn't well. With a tiny voice the little girl asks "Is grandma ok?"

Henry replies back while wiping his eyes "I'm afraid not this time pumpkin." Henry is a good father and does his best to make sure Lucy doesn't feel left out of any conversation no matter how difficult it may be.

"Grandma, you have a little visitor."

As the light shines through the window you can see the tears well up in grandma's eyes. She turns and looks at the child now sitting on the edge of the bed. "How many years have I know you now Sherbert?" A nickname her grandmother gave her due to her red hair. "2 years now?"

The little girl giggles and replies "No.. 5 years grandma."

"Oh, 5 short years and we've.." During mid-sentence the woman's eyes grow wide and frightened as she now looks past the little girl, she screams "LORD HAVE MERCY!!"

Henry goes from a smile to an immediate look of concern "Mom what?"

"SWEET GOD!!! Make it go away!" She yells while starring directly into an empty corner. The woman flails back so hard that it knocks Lucy to the ground, she begins to cry and scream as well.

Two orderlies rush into the room pushing Henry aside, "Mrs. Davis there's nothing there, it's ok Mrs. Davis." They soothingly reply as they make sure her hands and feet stay constrained.

A Lawyer, Mr. Garrison, also enters the room to witness the commotion.

"Mrs. Davis now please don't fight us, we're making sure you don't hurt anyone let alone yourself." The orderlies politely confess.

Henry looks to Lucy and shoves her towards the lawyer and pleads with him "Please take her out of the room.. Please. Please."

The lawyer looks annoyed for even being bothered by this simple request. "C'mon lil lady, did you see they have comic books on the table?"

"Mom.. mom" Henry awkwardly says through the scurrying orderlies attempting to calm the frail woman with straps and belts. "Mom, I'll stop back by in the morning. Maybe we.. Maybe.."

The woman quickly catches eye contact with Henry and under muffled breath states "We didn't mean to hurt them." Henry looks confused. She says again "We didn't know what we were doing."

A woman nurse walks in and puts her hand on Henry's shoulder "Sir, maybe tomorrow might be better for you to come back and you can even.."

"Henry" the woman whimpers as they are tightening the straps. "Henry, don't leave me like this."

One of the orderlies assures Henry "She'll be fine Sir, we promise."

"Henry, we didn't know.. We didn't know."

Henry scoots in closer to his mom and asks "What mom? Didn't know what?"

The air becomes calm and his mother looks at him in the eyes with sadness and says "We didn't know what monsters we had become Henry. Not them, not them. It was us that were the monsters."

The woman sniffles and tears fill her eyes. "We ate them." "WE ATE THEM!"

Her head slightly nods up and down as Henry looks taken back. This suddenly feels like the most real his mother has ever been with him. All of his life he can't recall learning to ride a bike or even her helping him to his feet to say that it would be ok. But, this moment Henry was all in on these precious words. This is the closest connection he's ever felt as their eyes locked. Henry moved in closer.

"Uh huh.." She nodded again as if she believes that Henry knows what she means. "We ate them and they screamed."

Henry leans in as the nurse begins to pull on his arm "Mr. Davis, honestly she'll be much better after getting some rest if you could.."

"Henry, may god forgive me."

"Mom" Henry begs. "Mom, who did you eat?"
"The orderly begins to pull back on Henry's coat as he stands his ground. Through the straps the woman holds onto the bottom zipper of Henry's coat and clings to it

"Squid people", "Squid people," she whispers.

Henry pulls back and keeps starring at her with a bewildered look. It's odd of course, but to Henry there's something very familiar about those 2 words. He can't place it.

"Sir, if you don't mind" the nurse pulls again on Henry's coat and leads him out the door.

In the hallway awaits Henry's little girl, she's shaken up but tough. "Will grandma be ok?" She asks. Henry crouches down to her eye level and sweeps back a strand of her hair that has fallen over her right eye. This time he doesn't say anything, he's holding in the shock of the last few moments. He simply gives her a reassuring smile back then stands up.

"Mr. Garrison, I can't thank you enough for helping me out. I think I'd like to try it again tomorrow if you don't mind."

Mr. Garrison sternly replies "Listen Mr. Davis, I don't think this is going to work out. I have other clients and I just don't think this is going to happen the way you think it will. I've seen these exact same moments a million times. The kids keep thinking that there's a pot of gold at the end the rainbow and once you get to those final moments.. You only realize you're left with funeral costs, memories and of course lawyer fees."

Mr. Garrison reaches into his coat and fumbles through a few business cards. "Here, if and when the time comes, call this number."

Henry tries to explain "But wait, how am I going to get the f.."

Mr. Garrison interjects with force "Henry, I will be sending you a bill for the sum of $650. Now, I doubt you can even afford that. Your mother signed over the farm, car and entire 23 acres to the church 14 years ago. She even included her extensive collection of ceramic figurines. Right down to the last detail."

Mr. Garrison moves in closer to Henry "Clearly she never had you in mind. I personally think it's a shitty ass thing that you're trying to do and I want no part of it." Mr. Garrison grabs his brief case and hat. He gives one last glance down to Lucy and walks down the hallway towards the outer doors.

Henry looks down and Lucy and gives a reassuring smile.

It was 2 days later that Henry would get the call from one of the nurses that his mother passed away. No fanfare, no goodbyes or lengthy conversations. Simply that she was gone and that the church would be calling on Tuesday to let him know when the funeral would be. After 35 years Henry, an only child, was feeling alone for the first time. Of course he had his wife and darling Lucy. But, this would be the first time ever that the people that raised him were no longer within a phone call or a visit. Even though Henry and his mother had grown apart over the last few years, there was still that bond of a mother and son. The memories were there, just not the deep love that he once knew as a child.

Shortly after the call Henry shared the news about grandma with Lucy and she cried late into the night. A deep sobbing cry that he never heard before. As he laid next to her to comfort her, he felt nothing for his mother. The only sorrow he felt was that of his daughter hurt. Only time.

Chapter 2 – Do something, anything

A small modest house on the edge of a cornfield we hear the evening crickets and neighbors talking. The smell of a pot roast fills the neighborhood air as Henry finishes up with the dishes. Lucy sits at the dining room table and gives out a long hard yawn. As she smacks her lips she asks "Dad?"

Henry quickly yells out "I love you more!"

"HEY!" Lucy says with a frown as if she's been beaten to the punch. "I was going to say that."

"I know tomato head" Henry says with a laugh.

"You can't say it before I say it." Lucy states. "That's not the rules."

Henry smiles, takes the damp dish towel off his shoulder, looks out the kitchen window. He notices car lights passing across the yard, his wife is returning home from a long day of work. Without turning around he whispers to Lucy "Psst, put the iPad away and grab a book before mom comes in the door, stat?" Lucy scurries off the table, plugs in the iPad to the charger then grabs a book.

The door comes opens and Lucy blurts out "Mom, dad says we're getting another dog?"

Both Henry and Angie lament back "WHAT? What?"

Lucy simply laughs as Angie closes the door behind her and takes off her jacket "I can't even get in the door and you're talking about another dog?"

Lucy explains "well, I just figured that Mr. Nibbles was lonely and he needed a friend, a brother? A pal to spend his days with."

Henry looks across the room at Angie, they make eye contact as she takes off her scarf.

Angie says "Well, honey.. Daddy's home with Mr. Nibbles all day, so. I highly doubt that he's lonely at all.."

Henry, looks down to the floor as he takes the dish towel off his shoulder and places it on the counter. You can tell he's embarrassed that Angie is the only source of income in the family. Henry had a steady job as an editor at the Mason City Globe Gazette for 15 years. But, 2 years ago he gave that up to explore writing a book. Henry has numerous notes and ideas laying around the house, but an actual chapter or even an outline never came to light.

Only a dream and numerous hours pacing the floors, watching movies and mowing the lawn. Somewhere along the way people will say that Henry got lazy, for sure his in-laws are steady reminder of this information. But, not for Henry. It's not about being lazy it was always about belief that he could do it.

He looks back on the days he left his job at the Gazette, so sure of himself and so full of confidence. OR was that only what he sold himself into believing? Was it the idea of a major book deal with a famous publisher? Maybe even a movie deal where someone famous would play his lead character and you'd see them one day accepting an Oscar and sending their gratitude to him. To Henry.

Or was it Henry's contempt for what others think of as a normal job? Stability? How can anyone live on paycheck to paycheck and be fine with that, Henry thought. Just enough money to pay for the car, groceries and daily life. But, that's it. The next thing worse would be to wake up an 82 year old still living in the same house, same car, same everything. And never once leaving this shitty town. It was a trap. A life sentence that none of us ever realized we signed up for. But, we're consigned to it. Most people are very content within the walls of this world. Then, there's Henry.

Angie enters the kitchen "Sooo, Lucy what can you tell me about The Art of Zen?" Lucy looks up at her mom with squinty eyes as if her mom is trying to quiz her. Henry sets a plate of food in front of Angie and looks towards Lucy as well.

"Do you find that good bed time reading? Or was it the fastest thing you could grab before putting your iPad away?" Angie asks as she glances down at the book. Lucy flips over her book to notice that it's Sun Tzu and not one of her own books. She looks back at her mom and they both give a good heart-felt laugh.

Later in the evening Lucy steps out of the bath and Henry helps her with a towel "Alright fluff ball. Hurry up, get dried off and hit the hay. School in the morning and we're not missing the bus this time. I've gotta run out to Grandma's farm and pick up a few things that the church said I could have."

As Lucy fluffs her hair she asks her dad "If you see any pictures of grandma could you please ask the nice people if I can have one? Please?"

Henry nods his head. "Yup. Now, get your night light on and I'll come in and check on you in a bit. I'm going to talk with your mom a bit." Henry makes his way downstairs to find Angie sitting on the back porch with a beer in hand.

"I love the smell of fall" she says as he sits in a chair next to her. "It's the best season by far. Not too hot, not too cold. And that smell of the leaves." She soaks it in and takes a sip of her beer.

Henry asks "Do you have one of those for me?"

Angie quips back "Working yet?"

"HOLY SHIT ANGIE!" Henry loudly whispers as to not wake or startle Lucy laying upstairs. "Why won't you ever let up? I'm trying. I just lost my mother and I'd like to at the least get past these next few weeks if that's ok with you?"

"No Henry." Angie exclaims, "No you're trying to get past the rest of your life without doing a fucking thing. Your mom knew it. Your dad knew it. This whole fucking town knows it."

Henry goes quiet and looks out across the fields of dying corn and fireflies dancing. Maybe she's right he thinks. Deep down Henry has always believed that he's a failure at some level. Perhaps he's only been fooling himself and needs to wake up and not let go of what is right in front of him. Even if had to work at the local convenience store that's still honorable. At least there's a paycheck coming in.

Henry calmly explains "Listen, I know this has been a crap fest of a life for you. I understand that. There's nothing I can do to take back the last few years and I appreciate how hard you've busted your ass for what we have. I got us into this. Me."

Angie interrupts "Just to be clear, I don't give a shit about the past 2 years. That can never be undone. Everything I've done is for our daughter. Everything. Now I need you put your big boy pants on, stop with the poor me drama and step the fuck up. What did you think would happen Henry?" Angie stands up and walks to the porch railing. "Did you think that after you quit your job you'd become some famous writer and it would be happily ever after? Dude. Even writers have to keep writing. You were hoping for a one and done and ride off into the fucking sunset weren't you?"

She takes the last sip of her beer and says "When we first met Henry, you had all these dreams about being famous. We'd stay up all night talking about you. Just you! Now, after 15 years I'm finding out that you're in love with the idea of being famous. Not the actual work you have to put into it."

Henry stands up as well and starts to walk to the back door to head inside the house.

"Right on cue" Angie laughs. "When things get tough poor little Henry can't deal with it. Go ahead. Run away little boy."

Henry stops in the door way and slightly looks back, never making eye contact. He continues in as the screen door slams behind him. Angie returns to her seat and opens another beer. The house lights turn off for the night.

Chapter 3 – Unwanted memories

You can hear the sound of the gravel kicking up against the side of the pickup truck as Henry drives down the road. It leaves a huge wave of dust in the air that sweeps over the country fields. On the drive Henry can't help but feel nervous about the next few hours. The church called the other night to let him know that they have found a few of his mother's personal belongings and they didn't feel right about keeping them. And they felt even more guilty about throwing them out. After all, these weren't their memories. They didn't know what to do, and to be honest, they found it just as awkward as Henry did that his mother gave them everything in the end.

Up ahead you can see a small figure waving from under a tree at Henry. Almost as if the Pastor knows that this will be hard and he only wants to make Henry feel comforted in these moments.

Henry turns right into the small farm lot, the potholes in the gravel are so large that it shakes the cab of the truck as he slowly drives over them. The Pastor eagerly walks towards the truck to greet Henry.

"Hello Henry, hello. I'm glad to see you my boy."

Henry smiles as he exits the truck "Hello father, how are you."

The Pastor replies with a warm hand shake "I'm good, I'm good. I gave a baptism this morning and you won't believe it but the little guy peed all over my robe." They both laughed as the Pastor continues "Obviously at the time it wasn't funny, but since this morning I've found it quite amusing. And it wasn't a little pee, I mean it was a full gusher."

The Pastor moves in closer to place a hand on Henry's shoulder to comfort him as he finishes his story "I guess I never knew that a babies bladder could hold so much fluid. How are you Henry?"

Henry gazes out over the farm that he once lived on "I'm good father. Feels weird standing here now." Henry closes the truck door and begins walking towards the farm house with the pastors hand on his back.

"Well, this won't take long Henry" the pastor says. "I came across a few boxes of things and I just felt down right foolish for even having to be the one to decide what to do with them. I mean. This whole thing is just as uncomfortable for me as well as I'm doubly sure, for you." The pastor holds the screen door open as Henry pushes open the door that enters the kitchen.

Henry surveys the room as he walks in and it's almost as though he's stepped back into time. Everything feels the exact same as it did when he was a little boy growing up. Same curtains with the same cigarette burns from his father's habit. Same coffee table and the exact same butter dish that he believes they once won at the Iowa State Fair in one of those coin toss events.

"Well, I'd say your mother didn't believe in upgrading, no offense." The pastor sarcastically mumbles.

Henry responds "no, no she didn't. I don't think she cared much about anything after Pops died. It was as though her world just stopped."

Henry walks further into the house. "Tell you what Henry, I've gotta take a call. Take your time, look around and I'll be outside when you're done."

The pastor opens the door then points back "Oh yes! Those boxes I was talking about are on the chair there in the corner. I didn't look through them as it didn't feel it's any of my business. Let me know when you're ready and I'll come back in and lend a hand carrying them out, alright?"

Henry thanked the pastor and then quickly returned to his exploration of the house he once knew. His hands touch the wall paper that he remembered his mother and father putting up one year. The hallways see so small compared to when he was little. Almost as if the house had shrunk. There was always a damp smell throughout the house due to the basement always flooding in the spring time. Henry stops in front of the steps leading up to the upstairs bedrooms. He felt weird about how silent the house was and almost scared at what he would find in his old room. Would it still be just as he left it or had his mother turned it into a craft room? He recalled sliding down the stairs in a cardboard box as a kid and how hard his dad would laugh and how loud his mother would cry out how he would break his damn fool neck. With his courage built up Henry makes his way up the 2 flights of worn wooden stairs. At the top he walks slowly and is amazed at how small the rooms seemed. He remembered awaking on his birthday mornings and presents awaiting him in this small mid-hallway.

    Every step, with every familiar creek of the floor boards, memories come flooding back in. Instead of inspecting his old room Henry decides to continue into his parent's room. The smell was the same. After 40+ years of living on the farm his mother never changed the dynamics of the room. The dresser and bed were never rearranged. They were exactly where Henry remembered them. He could literally walk the house blind-folded and not bump into a single furnishing or object.

As Henry stands in his parent's door way he thinks back on a hiding spot he once had. Just beyond the closet there use to be another room. Back in the day, closet space wasn't a factor when building a home. So, in order to make more space people would wall off gable in order to make a make-shift closet. Sacrificing natural light for places to hide more things.

   Henry marveled at this memory and he wondered if his mother hid anything back there not knowing that he would be the one to find it one day. What sort of treasures awaited him? Would it be a box full of much needed cash? Or even some jewelry that he could pawn.

Henry peeks from the upstairs window to spy on the pastor's doings. Just as expected the pastor is still on the phone chatting. Henry quickly darts back to the closet door in search of treasure. Once in the closet Henry has to crawl on his stomach to the hidden room behind the closet. Once there he's completely amazed at the number of items yet untouched. They hadn't found it, he thought with joy. This was new territory, but he knew he had to be quick. This would after all be his last visit to the home and he needed to cover as much ground before the pastor became aware of his whereabouts.

As Henry looked over each of the items he was shocked at how mundane some of them were. An egg beater and bowls for example seemed extremely out of place for a hidden closet. Some of the items were clothes and some were old toys that he once played with. Towards the back Henry discovers a box with notebooks and his mother's writings. In some of the notebooks it isn't his mother's handwriting but perhaps his grandfather's handwriting. He only thinks this because there's also many newspaper clippings of WW2 and photos of his grandfather in military uniform. One of the journals has some papers falling out of it and Henry notices sketches. The detail of some of the sketches were amazing. Looks like grandpa was one heck of an artist, he may have missed his calling. The sketches were of buildings, street corners and landmarks. There's even a sketch of what he believes to be his mother as a child. There's also an address in the bottom right corner reading Crown Heights, Brooklyn.

Just then Henry hears a voice from the kitchen.

"Henry? Are you up there?"

Henry hastily pulls together the pages of the notebook and rushes to the closet in hopes of not getting caught by the pastor.

"Henry? I'm coming up if that's ok?" The pastor yells from the bottom of the steps. Henry stuffs the notebook into his waist and crawls as quickly as he can to get back into the closet. He can hear the pastor's footsteps slowly coming the steps, he recognizes those creeks and knows he doesn't have much time. "Henry?" The pastor nervously asks as he walks up the steps. "Are you up there?"

Henry gets to the closet and is completely covered in dust. Just then then pastor opens the door to the bedroom and asks "Henry, are you in here? I thought I heard.."

" Yup! Yup!" Henry replies standing in the closet. "Ya know. Ya know, I swear to god I heard a bird or a bat in here." The pastor looks Henry up and down in astonishment of how much dust is caked onto him. Even in his eyebrows. Henry continues "I mean, not god, sorry father. I mean I just wanted to make sure there wasn't a hole in the ceiling with winter coming. Shall we head out father? I think I'm done here."

As the two men walk out carrying the small boxes Henry looks back towards the gable peak wondering what else might have been back in that hidden room. Does it matter? Or, will the thought of what might be in there haunt him forever.

"Say Henry" the pastor brings up. "I've found a family looking to live here and they'd like to move in right away. I hate that this is even happening to either of us but I just wanted you to know that.."

"It's fine father" Henry adds. The pastor doesn't say another word and places his box on the passenger side of Henry's truck then closes the door.

Chapter 4 – Terms of discovery

Henry returns home and is happily greeted by Lucy in the drive-way. She's apparently been riding around the block for hours waiting for her father to get home with news of the farm visit.

"Well, look at what the cat dragged in daddy-O." Lucy says with a bit of a southern twang. "How'd it go?"

Henry can barely get his truck door open as Lucy stands there on her bike. "Good" Henry says. "As good as it could have gone frog face."

Lucy whines back "Hey, how dare you say that to this little face tomato toes."

Henry grabs one of the boxes to bring into the house and laughs at Lucy's retort. "Tomato toes" he laughs. "Now that's one I haven't heard in a long time, but I'm positive it's the proper term for my toes." He says in an English accent.

"Dad! What do you get when you cross a toad and a raccoon?"

"Well, that very much sounds like a toe-coon or possibly a rack-oad" Henry replies.

Lucy laughs in astonishment and asks "HOW DO YOU DO THAT?!? Ok, ok.. How about a whale and a baboon?"

Henry simply replies "Well, a whack-oon of course, duh!?" The two laugh as they enter the house and Lucy keeps throwing animal combinations at him with the oddest results. Henry always has an answer.

Later into the night Henry's curiosity keeps him awake on the couch. The drawings were incredible and so well done, he wondered what else his grandfather had possibly drawn from those days. Henry clicks on the light and brings the journal to the couch to inspect further. As he rummages through each page he finds similar sketches as before, pencils of people from grandpa's hometown of Brooklyn, NY and yet the sketch of Henry's mom. Sketch after sketch has such detail and shading that the images pop off the page. Some are a bit over exaggerated as if grandfather was toying with shapes and images. Then, as Henry gets to the middle of the stack he's caught off guard by a very unique image. It's a sketch of a squid-like creature in a cage set in the corner of a room. Henry's eyes widen. He blinks a bit with disbelief. He turns the page and there again is another sketch. This one much closer to the subject. It's outlining the detail of a squid-like creature with human looking eyes. His grandfather even drew in the details of the blood vessels running across the place where an eyebrow would be. Is this it he wondered? Henry runs over and turns on the main living room light to get a better look at his discovery. As he keeps digging he turns up more and more of these remarkable renderings. Each one from a different angle and each with exquisite detail. The subject had to be real he thinks as his eyes widen. These are not simply just some random school drawings for fun or on a whim. These look like actual captive subjects. Melancholy subjects at that. Henry looks closer into one of the images and he sees that one of the creatures sits in front of a small audience. Someone is even holding up a bidding card in the very front of the seating. The room looks dark and sinister like a chamber deep in a basement.

Early the next morning, Henry awakens to find Angie standing over the journal sketches strewn across the floor. He can see in her expression that these illustrations sicken her to the core. She casually looks each one of them over and asks "Where did you find these Henry?"

Henry sits up on the couch and says "It seems as though my grandfather was an artist."

" I'd say a sick artist" she answers back with a negative tone. "Where did you find them at?"

Henry gets up from the couch and heads towards the kitchen. "I went to the farm yesterday to grab a few items that the church didn't know what to do with. Deep in a back closet I found those." Henry pours himself a cup of coffee. Angie continues to look over the sketches with disgust. Suddenly Angie starts shuffling the sketches into a pile as she hears Lucy's feet coming down the steps for breakfast.

Henry distracts Lucy with a "Good morning fuzz face. You hungry? Pancakes sound good or an egg?" As Angie shuffles the papers together and stuffs them back into the journal.

"I was thinking about pancakes Allll night." Lucy says.

Henry glances back into the living room as Angie looks back at him, still stashing the sketches in a drawer. "Pancakes it is... one or two?"

"Two please. In the shape of a cat!" Lucy adds.

Henry laughs "I'm allergic to cats but I'll see what I can do. I was thinking more like a ball shape. Round. Circular or as some would say a sphere." Lucy laughs.

As Henry prepares the pancakes he openly starts a discussion "Hey team, I was thinking about the past week or two about travelling back to where my grandfather grew up." Angie enters into the kitchen with a discontent look on her face. She leans against the door jam.

Henry notices the look as Lucy blurts out "Wasn't he from Des Moines or something?"

Henry laughs and corrects her "Brooklyn, NY actually. A long ways from here."

Angie chimes in "Sounds expensive." Henry sprays a hot pan with butter spray and ignores the comment.

Lucy asks "Brooklyn, NY? How many days will it take you to get there? You flying?"

Henry replies "Actually I was thinking about driving" as he pours the pancake batter into the pan. "It'll only be a week or so and I'll be right back."

"Whatcha gonna do there? Where will you sleep dad?" Lucy asks with a silly voice.

"Well, I'm not sure Lucy but I know it's something I'd like to do for us and especially Grandma."

As Henry slides a pancake onto Lucy's plate he glances up to make sure Angie is listening and says "And ya know what? I'm on a fact finding mission about a new book I'm writing."

Angie rolls her eyes as Lucy says with excitement "Ooh! I can't wait to read it. What's it about daddy."

Henry responds "Well, it's top, top, top secret at the moment sweetie. But, I'm positive it'll be a smash hit!"

"OH MY!" Lucy exclaims with a truly genuine look of excitement on her face. Henry gets animated as he slides another pancake onto Lucy's plate "It's got chills! It's got thrills!"

Angie pulls out a chair and sits across from Lucy. Henry asks "Want a pancake Ang?"

Angie has been examining her phone the past few minutes and she states "You do realize that Brooklyn is over 1,000 miles away from here right? And in your clunker of a crap truck? The gas alone will be.."

Henry interrupts with a wink to Lucy "Totally worth it!" Angie looks up in astonishment as Henry just plays off the seriousness of her concern. Henry asks again "Want a pancake? I can make them in the shape of a Death Star?"

Angie replies with a very curt tone "No fuck head, I want you to grow up a bit and come back to reality. Do you even realize that we're flat broke?" Lucy looks shocked at how her mom is speaking to Henry and Henry is just as concerned that Lucy is witnessing this moment.

Henry speaks "Hey, maybe we should talk more in private about this and work things out before we.."

Angie interrupts again with a look that could kill. "Lucy, if it makes you feel better you can eat your breakfast on the porch otherwise you're more than welcome to join me in reality here. Henry, we are broke! Your little hiatus has put us in debt with everyone including the school. I'm not even sure we have enough money in Lucy's lunch account for the next 3 days let alone the school year. And what is this amazing top secret idea you have that requires you to burn up gas money and drive all the way to Brooklyn for fucks sake? Care to share your extraordinary idea with the rest of the class Henry? Do you have a job there? Did someone hire you to travel there and are paying for this adventure? Did you find buried treasure in the backyard Henry and just so happen to forget to tell me about it?"

Angie lights up a cigarette in the house for the first time ever and continues. "Do you know many nights I have dreamed about telling those bitches at the Wharf to go fuck themselves? Huh? Like every single night Henry. Yeah! I bust my ass for you to sit at home and watch TV and mope."

Lucy shyly begins to get up from the table as Angie sternly says "Sit you little ass back down." Angie points her hand with the cigarette towards Henry and adds "Lucy, this is why." She exhales her breath of smoke "This is why you don't marry for love." The room gets quiet as she sits back in her chair and looks directly at Henry with scorn. She takes a quick drag and says "Love is nothing but a fucking sugar high then all you're left with is the garbage and remnants of broken promises."

Angie exhales her smoke again purposefully drawing attention to the no smoking in the house policy. Henry and Lucy remain still as though they're waiting for the storm to pass. Neither of them can even form a word or a facial expression for fear of how much more enraged she might become. Staying silent is sometimes safer.

"So Henry, here's the deal." Angie grabs her pack of cigs and stands up from the table. "You get in that truck and go get a job by the end of this week. Or, you get in that truck and go to New York. One of these paths makes complete sense to me. You're a big boy Henry." As Angie walks into the living room and packs up for work. The air is still silent, Henry is still holding the pan and spatula as the front door slams shut.

Henry looks at Lucy as she looks back with saddened concerned expression on her face. Her messy morning hair shines from the sunlight coming through the window. Henry says "Well, I guess she didn't want a pancake." And they both give out a huge laugh and Lucy continues to finish her breakfast. Henry places the pan in the sink to rinse it off but you can see in his face that he's troubled by this hard decision he needs to make. Not because his wife is mad or anything, but what will it mean for Lucy. Will she be ok? Will she treat her kindly over the next week in his absence? He loves her beyond words.

   Later that afternoon Henry thought very hard about what Angie had said about their financial situation. She's right. She has been supporting the family for the past 2 years.

As upset as Henry was about her little blow up earlier, he knew she was right. No need to argue that point. He couldn't allow this one last dream to be a burden on Lucy. This is his one last shot at proving himself to everyone, to Angie and especially himself. If those sketches represented anything remotely real once upon a time. This could be the biggest story ever. So Henry came up with a sound plan to sell the truck and use the money to offset the cost of a bus ticket, food and possibly even a cheap hotel room for a few nights. If he can get enough money from the deal it might even guarantee him a ride home. An incredible story about a squid man, he thought, would guarantee a flight home first class. That would be amazing.

Henry knew exactly who to call first about the truck. The pastor. He knew that the pastor was a good man deep down and perhaps maybe he could play off of his guilt to get top dollar for the truck. After all, the church just received over $750,000 according to Henry's calculations. Heck, their neighbor's parents just sold 14 acres for $8,000 an acre last year. He was sure that the pastor could part with $1,800 in exchange for the truck. So Henry gave him a call and threw out his asking price of $1,800. The pastor, did sound a bit sheepish on the phone but agreed to purchase the truck but for $1,100. It was something. Henry agreed and would meet him in the following morning.

Chapter 5 – Follow the footage

During the night Henry couldn't sleep. It was a long day and there was a ton of emotions going on at the same time. Excited about his new mission and adventure but also very nervous. Not only about the trip and what he might find. But, about leaving behind Lucy. Since Henry was also an only child, he had a deep bond with Lucy. He knew how lonely she would be without him home to make her laugh. He knew how she worried about him even when he went to the grocery store. Or, like the time he shoveled the drive way last winter and she made him hot chocolate because she didn't want him to catch hypothermia. It sounded much funnier when she said that word. Plus, he gave her high praise for even knowing when and where to use that word.

Henry decided to turn on his laptop and do a bit of research online about squid-like creatures or octopus man. Just trying to find something, anything that could back up the drawings. Up came an old cartoon came up about squid people dancing. Of course there were numerous videos of people being silly and wearing octopus hats, but deep into a few links things got sinister and odd.

One of the video links from an article showed what appeared to be a squid like man. It had legs and for sure arms because they were raised up in a defensive posture and were bound in rope. The old 16 mm looking footage was very damaged, it was a recording of a recording, but Henry could clearly hear the creature whimpering.

Whoever was holding the camera and filming took great joy in this things suffering. Henry's eyes are squinting at the laptop screen in the dark. He's both blinded by the light as well as unnerved by what's he's witnessing. It's gruesome. It's sickening. He occasionally turns down the volume as to not wake anyone in the home. The whimpering and taunts alone make Henry wince.

   Once in a while Henry hits pause on the video only to turn his head sideways and try and make out the creatures distinct features. Is this real he wondered? Is this just a hoax like those old alien videos everyone has seen from the Roswell incident? Or, was this some sort of 1950's film student's work? It can't be fake, he thinks.

The footage is so poorly done that it only adds to the authenticity. And for what? There's been some odd videos out there with people doing wacky shit. But, this.. this was something that Henry has never witnessed before.

   Henry looks down at the video author, video likes and the date it was published. It reads Moseley. The date published was only 5 years ago and there were only 16 likes. Which means, not very many people have seen this. Henry quickly scans the video details section and decides to send an email to video author. What should it say? "Hello, my name is Henry and I'm fascinated with your awkwardly creepy video from 5 years ago? Kindly email me back because I'm not mental?" Of course not.

So Henry begins to carefully craft his email as it starts, "I'm very sorry to trouble you and this may seem a bit odd. I am responding to the origination of your squid man video dated 5 years ago. It is very gruesome and I would just like to know the background of the footage. Was this a school film project? Or was it just a prank? Either way I am interested in your story. I will be travelling over the next week so please forgive me if I don't respond right away. Thank you for your time, Henry." Henry's hand hesitates as he prepares to hit send on the email. So odd of a request but, based on the sketches by his grandfather and the last words he heard from his mother this was the next best clue he had.

Before the girls could awake Henry peeked into each of their rooms. In his wife's room he placed a letter in an envelope simply titled Ang. In it he apologized for all of the troubles he felt that he brought upon her. He hoped she would forgive him for this one last quest. This one chance to make things right. One last dream. He also wrote that he still loved her very much. It wasn't hard for him to write it as much as he knew it would trouble her to read it. He didn't think she felt the same anymore and in a way Henry understood that she was only there to keep up a normal appearance for Lucy. He signed it "Your person" just as a subtle reminder of how they felt about each other when they first met. He knew this might be a small dig at the situation, but.. He was hoping that maybe they would work things out. To him she was still beautiful.

As Henry walked to Lucy's room he could hear her shuffling in her bed. He crept quieter as to not wake her. Henry had tears in his eyes as the he looked over her sleeping and he knew that a conversation would only stop him from ever leaving. This was the hardest part. He pulled up the blankets tighter over her shoulder to keep her warm. On her desk he placed the sketch that his grandfather drew of his mother. She had once asked him for a photo of grandmother and this was the best he could do. He placed a little note on the upper right corner reminding her that this was her Grandmother and that she loved her Sherbert very much. And that she would always be looking down on us. Henry's eyes begin to flood with tears, he quickly turned away from it all and headed downstairs and out the back door.

Chapter 6 – Heading Eastward

The bus ride was actually very relaxing for Henry. It was a time to put aside the death of this mother, the farm and all of the troubles he felt he had been creating for the family. Right now at this very moment there was nothing he had to do but ride and wonder. Everyone talks about how flat Iowa is, but this way heading east, it's actually very hilly. Especially once you hit Davenport. Lots of valleys and drop offs. Every now and then, as Henry crosses over valleys he can see where old train bridges once stood. Now, just big cement pillars in the middle of a river. It was a dry summer so the water is very low. Too low to even canoe like he did as a boy with his dad. When he got older, he and his friends would go tubing down the river near Boone Iowa.

Occasionally even in some of those years the water was so low that he and his friends would have to stop on a sand bar and carry their canoes to running water again. Those were great days. Funny how as a teen the summer heat didn't matter as much as it does as an adult.

Henry's mind keeps going back to Lucy. He doesn't have a phone and he wouldn't know what to say to her at this moment besides that he missed her and he hoped she enjoyed the picture of Grandma. His eyes well up again. But, he's determined that what he's doing will make her life better. All of their lives better. This just has to work.

The bus seems to make frequent stops along the way in little towns with names he's never heard in his entire life of being born and raised in Iowa. How odd, he thought, living in Iowa and not being aware that these little towns even existed. Nobody gets on and nobody gets off the bus except for the driver at each stop. Henry laughed to himself believing that maybe the driver has a bladder issue? Or a snack attack every hour on the hour. Earlier he noticed that the driver brought back corn chips and a huge burrito. You know, one of those kinds that you heat in the microwave for 30 seconds and it's suddenly scorching hot to even carry to the counter. He wondered why their microwave at home didn't heat with that type of ferocity. Heck, simply reheating a hot pocket at home for a full minute was worthlessly lukewarm.

As the driver approached the bus Henry stood up to ask a question. Others around him looked at him in shock for a second. As if it were unthinkable to actually move on the bus or ask to use the restroom now that the driver was coming back on. The bus door opens and Henry asks "Excuse me sir, what's our arrival time look like for our bus change in Chicago?" The bus driver doesn't even answer and proceeds to place his large pop into the cup holder. Henry begins to think that maybe he didn't hear him. He looks around at the other faces on the bus with a smirk because he knows this time he has to ask again but louder. This should be good "excuse me Sir but.. "

The bus driver spins his head towards Henry with a look of annoyance, "3 hours" he says. Like he should already know that. And to be honest, maybe he should have. The bus driver buckles in his seat belt and peers at Henry through the rearview mirror. Henry decides to sit down. Again he looks around at the few others on the bus with a smile. Iowans are polite most of the time. Unless you're undecided on a college team, driving in their lane or holding up the bus.

Over the next few bouncy hours Henry had dozed on and off. His thoughts were filled with delusions of grandeur about his new book idea. What will he find once he got to Crown Heights? Where will he start? It's not like there will be any signs along the way that say "squid creatures right this way" or anything. All he had were the sketches and a vague address.

Henry suddenly remembered the email that he sent and wondered if there had been a reply yet. He pulled open his backpack and pulled out the laptop. Sure enough. Bam. One reply from a Moseley Williams. He readjusted the laptop, took a small breath and clicked on the email. It read "Hello, thank you for your interest in the video. I assure you that it's no hoax. I have an entire box of old 16 mm footage in my basement that seem to be from the 1950's and I'd be willing to sell them. Each film is just as disgusting as the next. Please let me know if you're interested or not as I have another buyer waiting. Moseley."

Wow! Here we go Henry thought. One minute grasping at straws the next possibly a direct connection to the source. Without hesitation Henry eagerly hits reply "Thank you Moseley for your quick response. I am actually on the road heading to New York as I type but would love the opportunity to look over each of the films and make you a fair offer."

Henry's lying of course, but he has to find some way to stall this pending purchase from another buyer. He continues "Where are you located and possibly I could swing by within a day or two to take the films off your hands. I'm very excited to learn that there's more than one film besides the one online. I would, however, like to inspect the remaining films to ensure quality. I hope you don't mind. Henry."

Henry can't even believe this very moment is happening. Not only has he found a solid lead to the squid people, but there's multiple videos. Multiple. In a box. And disgusting no less.. Henry lifts his head and looks out the window with wonder. He thinks that if he can simply view and inspect the footage he won't have to purchase them at all. He just needs more to go on. Validation that these squid people exist and that his grandfather's drawing are somehow linked. Where did the videos come from? Was there a connection? There were just too many similarities for this to be a coincidence. Never once in his life has he seen or heard of anything like these creatures.

The bus got off the main highway a while ago and we've now travelling the city streets of South Chicago. Henry's email alert dings. His eyes are wide open in anticipation that Moseley is somewhere on the way or nearby. The email reads "Hello again Henry, I am located in Lakewood, Ohio."

    Henry opens another tab with lighting speed. Maps, Lakewood, Ohio. As the site reloads he learns that Lakewood is actually a small suburb just west of Cleveland. Henry grabs the bus schedule, scrolls down the list of bus stops with his finger and finds Sandusky, Ohio on the list. He looks up and thinks it over for a second. If he can get off in Sandusky maybe he can catch a cab or a city bus to Lakewood and be there by 9am tomorrow. And actually, one night stop in a hotel and some food sounded really good. He continues to read the email "Absolutely you can take a peek at the footage. But, please hurry as my other buyer is getting impatient. Please let me know your schedule and I can send you my full address once you get closer. I don't trust people and I just want to make sure I'm around the house if you get close. Thanks again. Moseley."

Henry replies "Moseley, we both got lucky actually. I'm actually staying in Sandusky overnight and can be at your place around 9am. Please email me your address let me know if that time works for you or not. Looking forward to it. Henry."

Somewhere between Michigan City and Sandusky Henry got the address and confirmation on the time. Moseley's email sounded promising and that the other bidder might not be in the area either. So, his chances were good. During the night Henry found a cheap hotel, it was right next to a cemetery but it was only $39, so it was totally worth the creepiness factor. Nothing else was really open so he grabbed a bag of chips and an orange juice from the vending machine. At first, the combination seemed like a bad idea but after a full day of travelling the orange juice was absolutely magnificently refreshing. And it gave him a sense that at least he at something healthy today.

As Henry lay on the crisp cool sheets of the bed he thought about calling Angie a couple times just to check in on Lucy. Just to see how her day was went. He'd reach for the phone then play out the conversation in his head. Each time he replayed it in his head it always came out negative. It would roll into money issues then into the topic of him getting a full-time job. He knew exactly where it would lead. And yet, he felt extremely guilty about not wishing Lucy a good night. Letting her know where he was at and that he would be home soon to play. The he also remembered the time. It was late on a school night and that would just give Angie one more reason to bitch.

Chapter 6 – Mosely's grandpa

Henry couldn't help but pop straight out of bed before the sun was even fully up. He's never ever been an early riser and would much rather sleep in until late mid-morning. But today was different and everything was lined up. He found a cab company that could pick him up at precisely 7:15 in the front entrance. That gave him plenty of time to grab the free breakfast, steal a couple extra slices of bread for the road, and throw down at least 3 cups of coffee. And obviously, hit the restroom before he got into the cab for the hour and half drive into the West side of Cleveland. It was truly incredible he thought, how just a few sketches and an odd video is now leading him to Cleveland, Ohio. He'd never even thought about Cleveland or ever dreamed of a reason to visit Cleveland. But this was it.

7:13 rolled around and right on time the cab rolled in. The driver didn't say much except quick one word answers like "yes sir" and "no sir." That's pretty much it. Henry even tried to make small talk along the way and yet the driver only nodded his head in agreement from time to time. Or, in most instances, completely ignored Henry. That's ok Henry thought, there truly wasn't any reason to make small talk other than just being polite. After all, they'd never meet up again in life. And who knows? Maybe the guy was just going through some personal issues and was using this time to reflect? Henry actually had more fun sitting in the back and concocting all the scenarios in his head on why this guy was so quiet. Right down to the plausibility that the driver was actually in the witness relocation program and was only being silent for the sake of saving Henry's life from mob bosses out of Atlanta. Henry smiled to himself. Maybe it was a good thing to not know what was going on. But, Iowan's are nosey like that. They call it neighborly.

The taxi rolled into Moseley's neighborhood around 9:10, Henry had never seen traffic like that in his entire life. Sheffield, Iowa was a completely relaxed vibe compared to that. Henry hoped that the timing would still be ok even though he was running late.

"Looks like it's up on the right" Henry reminded the driver.

The cab slowed down and puled to the right side of the quiet street. "That's be $52 please sir" the driver said.

"Here's and even $60. I hope you enjoy the rest of your day." Henry handed over the three $20 and exited the cab. Of course there was no big send off, the cab just took off as soon as the door was shut. Henry wasn't even sure that the door even fully slammed before the guy hit the gas, but oh well.

Henry looked back and forth on the street just getting a sense of what Cleveland was like and breathing in the air. He could smell the lake in the small breezes passing by. It was oddly relaxing compared to the smells of home and Turkey farms.

   3420, 3420 Henry kept saying over and over in his head as he looked over the house numbers trying to locate Moseley's address. 3420, and here it is.

   He whispered out loud "here we go."

Henry walked up the rickety 2 flights of wooden steps. It didn't seem as if Moseley cared much about the well-being of his home on the outside, he could only image what it was like on the inside. As he walked up the steps he would look up at the windows in the hopes as to not need to ring the doorbell. Hopefully someone would be just as anxious that he was arriving and would greet him at the door. He took his time with each step. Some of the windows had broken blinds and the curtains looked like something out of a 1960's hippy van. You know, those yellow yarn curtains that have the small dangly balls at the bottom. Henry was sure he was in for a real treat. Unfortunately, nobody had noticed his arrival and now came the decision of knocking or pressing in on the painted over doorbell.

Henry felt a knock was the most polite approach. He started with a light knock as to not startle anyone on the inside, and to assure Moseley that he was a normal stand-up guy and not some weirdo. Nobody answered. Just as Henry began his second series of knocks a loud yipping from small dog on the other side began. The dog sounded intense. You could hear it's little collar jingling and toenails scratching at the door. It didn't sound big enough to do any harm but you never know with small dogs. It's those little bites that hurt like crap.

The yipping continued until Henry heard a voice in the house yell out "Gypsy, get back." The dog doesn't seem to let up. "Gypsy, get back now" the voice repeats.

"Hello Henry, hold on one second." The door unlocks and opens. There stands a skinny teenager with a huge smile. Nothing at all like what Henry had expected to see.

"Hello, you must be Moseley then?

"Yes Sir, come in, please come in" the young man says.

Henry can't help but feel completely confused by this as he walks through the door. But, he's chomping at the bit to see the footage and inspect it's originality.

"Please take off your shoes and come on in."

Henry kicked off his shoes and looked around the house and wondered why he even bothered. It doesn't look like it's been cared for in years. Everything was very dated right down to the peeling wallpaper and antique furniture. Henry can hear the little dog trying to claw his way out from some other room in the back of the house. He's just thrilled he didn't have to face down the demon. He's sure he would have lost a toe.

"Well, you sure have a lovely house" Henry says as he extends out his hand to offer a shake to Moseley.

"Actually this is my grandparent's home." Moseley says as he leaves Henry's hand frozen in the air without even noticing.

"Come on downstairs, I have the stuff you're looking for all set up down there and ready to go." Henry starts to get very nervous about following a completely stranger he found on the internet into their basement. Of course his curiosity is peaked, but Henry's not about to make this easy for some serial killer to just end it like that. Why wasn't the box of films up here on the table? Why would they be in the basement if Moseley knew he was coming for them today? Lots of questions in Henry's head so he decides to stall a bit and feel out the situation.

"So, this is your grandparent's house huh?"

"Sure is" Moseley says. "Keep coming and I'll explain.

Henry, gets that odd feeling again and asks "So, is grandpa or grandma home or will they be.." Suddenly Henry is confronted by grandpa standing still in a doorway. He gets startled. "Oh, shit. Sorry sir.. I didn't see you."

The old man just stands there with his eyes wide open staring back at Henry. He doesn't move or make a sound, he just stands there. He looks very old and frail. His face is extremely wrinkly and Henry begins to think that maybe his mind is gone from the blank stare in his eyes.

Henry repeats "Sorry, I was just.."

"Come on Henry, keep coming this way" Moseley says as if acknowledging that his grandfather might not be in the right frame of mind. Henry looks towards Moseley and once again looks back at grandpa just standing there. It's the spookiest stare he's ever seen in his entire life. Some people can simply have their eyes open and stare but it's as though grandpa has a look of terror and it has frozen his face in that position. Henry lowers his eyes and follows Moseley to the kitchen then down the stairs to the basement.

"Keep coming, don't mind him. He's old." Moseley explains.

Henry continues down the steps. Once down there it's a whole different world. Moseley has created his own sanctuary down here it appears. Far different than what's upstairs. After seeing grandpa he doesn't blame him. The room is littered with chip bags and pops cans but it's a pretty cool set-up. 1990's band posters, a gaming system connected to a tv, a fold out bed and even a mini-fridge.

"So, I'm going to be asking $1,200 for all the films." Moseley blurts out.
"Plus, I'm selling my film projector and screen as well if you're interested" he says as he points to the projector and screen in the corner of the room all set up.

Henry looks over the room and says "Well, hold up Mose. Can I call you Mose?"

"Moseley."

"Sure thing. Moseley." Henry politely replies.

"I was actually hoping to view the footage and check it out before I agree to any price. I have no idea what kind of condition it could be in and I'm just being cautious. You understand, right?"

Moseley, stands there for a few seconds thinking over the terms. His eyes twitching back and forth a bit. Henry wants to add a comment in the awkward silence but he knows he needs to remain silent and try to gain the upper hand in the negotiation process.

Moseley takes in a deep breath and exhales slowly "Sure, fine. It's all sitting in that box on the table near the projector. Ever worked one of those before?"

"It's been a long time, can you get me started and I'll take it from there?" Henry adds as he eagerly walks towards the box with film canisters sticking out. From his vantage point there has to be around 12 cans. All of them look extremely vintage. This might be exactly what he was looking for.

Moseley walks over with Henry and shows him the process of placing the film on the projector and running the strip through to the second reel.

"Seems easy enough" Henry says with a reassuring voice.

Mosely leans in closer to Henry and says with stern voice. "So, the only thing I'm asking is to not play the sound. It's horrific Henry. I don't want to hear it again and I sure as heck don't want my grandfather hearing it. One other thing.

This isn't some video store that you can sit around for hours and order up some popcorn or anything. Just go through one or two films, pay me the money and get out. Deal?"

Henry looks Moseley in the eyes and just nods his head in agreement. He's been waiting for this moment with great anticipation and can't wait another second to see what he's got. According to Moseley the footage is horrific. That comment was only the icing on the cake of enticement.

Henry looks over the projector one more time to ensure he's got the film running correctly then flips the switch. It's not exactly as Moseley had described yet, but it was absolutely nothing like anything Henry has seen in his entire life. There they were, these squid like people.

A least 4 of them lined up against a wall with some people in military uniforms huddling them together with long blunt sticks. The squid people seemed very docile and never once fought back. Henry felt terrible for them as they appeared very timid. Their skin was very smooth and clammy. Two large eyes on either side of their heads looked around the room in fear. Every now and then someone from behind the camera would spray them down with a hose. They were exactly how Henry imagined they would look. Tall and skinny. From their heads down to their hips they were 100% squid-like. Henry couldn't tell if they had arms due to all of the tentacles, but for sure they had legs. They were walking almost like a human.

The footage goes black then a film clapboard appears setting a new scene. It reads PROJECT 119 and moves out showing a room full of military personnel seated in a large warehouse like room. Someone in the foreground is speaking towards the camera and Henry is dying to turn on the sound. But, he resists the urge. Within seconds two armed military police wrangle in a single squid creature into the center of the room. The guy giving the speech keeps prodding the creature but it doesn't seem to even react. It's as if the creature has accepted its fate of being a part of this freak show. Henry looks behind him to see if Moseley is watching this at all. For some reason Moseley isn't in the room. So Henry softly shouts out "Moseley?" To which nobody answers back. Henry turns back to the footage and decides that maybe he'll turn up the volume a tiny bit just to listen in on what the guy is saying. So far it's not as horrific as Moseley stated. Henry thought that maybe Moseley just couldn't stomach this type of material as well as he could. Just then the projector speakers gave out a ghastly paralyzing squeal. Henry quickly looks at the screen. To his shock, the man giving the speech began to slice open the creature right in front of the audience. Without a care. As if he was dissecting the thing alive. It wailed in pain as Henry fumbled to find the switch to turn off the sound. The creature was screaming for its life as the man casually cut off tentacles and placed them on a tray. This was unbelievable Henry thought. It wasn't hurting anyone. How morbid. Henry found the switch for the volume and power so he just hit them both to be sure.

"Uh, Moseley?!? I'm sorry about that. You down here?" Henry asks into the room. He doesn't hear anything so he moves closer to the stairs heading up.

"Moseley? Are you..

Standing at the top of the stairs is grandpa again. Staring down at him.

"Oops, sorry sir. You haven't happened to see Moseley have you?"

The grandfather's mouth slowly opens into what appears to be a scream but no sound comes out. It's terrifying to Henry. Just then he hears Moseley's voice coming from somewhere upstairs.

"Hey man, what happened? You done?" Moseley asks as if he didn't hear a thing. He places his hand on his grandfather's shoulders and escorts him into the living room away from Henry and the stairs.

"This way gramps. I don't want you to fall."

Henry continues upstairs and into the kitchen. He watches as Moseley walks grandpa to the upstairs bedrooms. His face still in terror as he looks back towards Henry.

"Hey, you wouldn't happen to have a phone would you?" Henry says as he tries to compose himself from the horror of what he's just witnessed. Moseley holds his finger up to his lips and continues walking grandpa up to his room. Henry can't yet grasp what he's just witnessed. He searches the kitchen cupboard for a glass. That was absolutely awful what they did to that thing. Nothing on this earth, no matter what, should be slowly dismembered like that. The guy seemed like it was nothing. Just another day on the farm it seemed. A long time ago he once watched his grandfather butcher a pig in the barn with the same nonchalant demeanor. That was also a memory he wished he could erase. Finally Henry finds the cleanest glass he can find and as he fills it up with water from the faucet he hears Moseley renter the room.

"Alright man, you happy with the footage? Got the money on you?" Moseley asks.

Henry replies "No, I don't have the money on me but I can.."

"Ah shit man. You knew you were coming here to buy these films and you didn't think to bring your wallet? This isn't a library dude where you can sign them out whenever you feel like. I thought we had a deal?"

"Listen" Henry calmly explains, "I can get you some of the money. I'm going through a tough time and I can only give you $300. That's it. I didn't know you'd be asking for so much for these."

Moseley walks directly up to be face-to-face with Henry in an aggressive manner. He looks deep into Henry's eyes.

"Look, I told you I have another buyer that wants these bad boys. So, if you don't have the money you're wasting everyone's time here. Right? Door."

Henry looks back into Moseley's eyes and he can tell he's pissed. He knows that Moseley is right though. He never intended to ever purchase the films he just needed to verify that he wasn't crazy. It was proof that his mother and grandfather could have possibly even been in the same room with these creatures at one time or another. As far as he was concerned he had the proof he needed. Obviously, it would be incredible to have the films to show Angie and to have as back up for future proof. But, for $1,200 he just couldn't swing that amount. And he for sure couldn't call home and ask Angie for it. Could you imagine what words would come out of her mouth at that request?

"I'm sorry I troubled you Moseley. I truly am. If you just let me grab my bag I'll be on my way."

Moseley, steps to the side and allows Henry to gather his things. Henry gives one last look back at Moseley standing in the kitchen as he exists the home. He doesn't say a word.

As Henry gets about a half a block away from the home he hears Moseley's front screen door slam shut. He looks back to see Moseley running down the steps and towards him.
Henry hollers towards him "Hey man! Hey! I said I'm sorry."

Moseley slows down as he gets closer.

"Nah, hey man. I'm sorry about that. You know I just hate seeing my grandfather like that. I apologize." Moseley says as he gets closer and catches his breath.

Henry seems stunned by the sudden switch in Moseley's attitude. He's witnessed this bipolar behavior with his wife over the years, but this guy turns on a dime. It was only five minutes ago when Henry feared for his safety in a strangers kitchen.

"Look, that was dumb" Moseley explains. "I want to tell you the truth Henry. There is no other buyer." Henry's shoulders drop as he squints his eyes towards Moseley.

"I know. I know. I'm dumb. But, here's the deal. Last week my dad asked me to come live with him in Tacoma. The trouble is, he said that it was up to me on how I got there. I need the cash Henry. I'll take anything at this point."

Moseley's head drops down as if he's embarrassed to have just shared this information with a stranger. It was a great story but Henry's not 100% convinced it's legit.

"If you're being honest then I'll be honest. I'm flat broke Moseley." Henry says with huff. "I found some sketches that my grandfather did and they lead me to find your footage. That's the only reason I'm here. Is just to validate that these creatures are real. Then I'm planning on writing a book. Heck, if I can get my hands on those films I'd settle for a documentary on the subject. I'll even cut you in Mose."

Slowly Moseley lifts his head. His eyes widen at what Henry just told him.

"Did you say sketches?"

Henry replies "Yeah, like an entire journal. I have them here in my bag if you'd like to see them."

"Dude. I have sketches too." Moseley replies.

"You're kidding me?" Henry shoots back.

"So, when I found the box of films in my grandparent's attic I also found a handful of sketches. Sketches of the squiddies, man. Hear me out. I can't say with any certainty, but I'm fairly confident that my grandpa was there. Like, there there. In the fucking room there. Maybe even holding the camera. I don't know."

Henry, just listening, can't believe his ears to what Moseley is saying. He thinks to himself as Moseley is rambling, I'm not alone in this. Here's even more proof and another believer to add to the cause. A couple days ago this was all just a big gamble now today he's on the verge of blowing the lid off a huge story. Maybe even a possible military cover-up. Pulitzer prize material. Henry looks up behind Moseley and realizes that smoke is coming from his home.

"Mose, is that.."

Moseley looks towards the house and yells out "Shit!"

They both make a mad dash for the house. Once inside they realize that the smoke isn't coming from inside, but it's coming from the backyard. Moseley yells out "Grandpa?! Where are you?"

Even Henry yells out "Grandpa? Are you in here?" As they make their way through the home, through the kitchen and onto the back porch. Henry almost runs into the back of Moseley as he suddenly stops in horror.

In the backyard grandpa is standing with a large can of lighter fluid burning the box with the films. Grandpa looks up towards the men standing there. He has a look of pure joy and yells out with a raspy voice "May god forgive me." As the two men stand there staring I horror of their discovery going up in flames.

Only Henry notices that grandpa is still squeezing too hard on the can of lighter fluid and it's leading a trail of flame directly to his legs. "GRANDPA!" Henry yells out just as grandpa's legs catch fire. The old man begins to shake with the pain of the flame and squeezes the can even more shooting lighter fluid everywhere. Suddenly the entire backyard is engulfed and grandpa is screaming in the middle of it.

The two men run towards grandpa guarding their eyes from the heat of the flames that seem to be everywhere. "Grandpa!!" Moseley yells out in desperation but he can't seem to get close enough to help put out the flames all over his body now. Henry looks towards the house and spots a hose laying loose on the ground. He runs towards it, grabs only the end and quickly turns on the water.

"Mose heads up!" He yells pulling the hose along behind him. Grandpa's body is still on fire as he's rolling around in pain. But the grass is now soaked from all the lighter fluid that its only making the situation worse. Henry fiddles with the hose head and finally a spray comes shooting out the end. He aims it towards grandpa's body.

"Moseley, grab his legs and pull him out of there!" Henry yells. Moseley reaches into the flames and pulls the limp body out towards a clear area. The pants are gone and the skin is blackened. Grandpa's shoes are melting and still smoking. His face isn't even recognizable. There's a blue flame still lingering around the body as Henry does his best to douse it out.

"Grandpa? Grandpa?" Moseley shouts with tears in his eyes. "This is so fucked up man."

Within minutes the fire department, paramedics and the police department come in and take over. Somehow through all of that flame grandpa is still alive and breathing. The paramedics load him up and hit the sirens on their way to the hospital. Moseley is inconsolably crying on the back porch.

    Henry just stands there emotionless in a daze as the police ask him question after question. How did it happen? What's your relationship to the old man? How do you know Moseley? He answers them without hesitation and as forthright as he can be.

Even he can't believe what has just happened. Was all of this his fault he wondered? What if he would have just stayed in Iowa and gotten that full-time job at the convenience store? Maybe grandpa would be in his recliner right now watching his favorite shows. Maybe he'd be home right now with Angie and Lucy making pancakes. The questions seem to go on and on for 20 minutes it seems until he hears Moseley's voice for the first time.

"Dude. Henry." Moseley says while sniffling. "Hey, I've gotta head to the hospital to be there for gramps until my sister gets there. I'm probably asking a lot but.. could you come with me until she gets there?"

At this point Henry is numb. All of the adrenaline has completely drained out of his body. The very last thing Henry wants to do now is face down Moseley's sister and rehash this morning's tragic events. He even runs through the scenario of Moseley's sister confronting him on why he was there and then slapping him in the middle of all the hospital staff. But, Henry does feel a bit to blame. Maybe that's what he deserves. Then he can catch a bus immediately tonight back home and put this entire thing behind him.

Henry swallows in order to get enough saliva to form a word. With a crackly voice he simply says "Yeah. I'll go."

At the hospital Henry finally got up the nerve to call Angie. Their conversation wasn't terrible but it also wasn't constructive. During the call Henry confessed that the entire thing was a big mistake and that he would be coming home within 24 hours. He never mentioned anything about the morning mishap or about the film footage he discovered. Deep down he had already promised himself that he would go to his grave never sharing this day with anyone. Ever. After an hour nap in the chapel, Henry hears Moseley calling his name. Barely awake Henry calls back "Mose, yeah man. I'm in here."

Moseley enters the chapel and sits down next to Henry "Hey Henry, I was afraid you left already."

"Nope, nope. Is your sister here yet?" Henry asks while looking back towards the chapel door.

"Yeah, she got here an hour ago" Moseley replies with a positive sound in his voice. "But, don't worry about her. Listen, I have something I want to give you."

Henry looking confused replies "No wait, I'm the one that should be.."

Moseley stops him with his had up. "No, it's all good. I've kept something in my wallet for the past four to five years and I'd like you to have it. I think it will help."

"Well, Mose I don't think that I can accept anything that you have. I mean, your grandfather almost died today man." Henry says with a sheepish tone.

Moseley says "Here. On one of the sketches I found an address and I kept it all these years. I figured that maybe I would go check it out myself one of these days. But, as you know I couldn't even afford to get to Tacoma.

Henry blinks his eyes a few times trying to get the sleep out. He holds the piece of paper that Moseley just handed him and he tries to get his eyes to focus. 4802 Bedford Avenue Crown Heights, NY.

"Now here's the thing" Moseley adds. "It's not like a major building or anything. I looked it up one time online. It's someone's apartment building."

Henry looks up at Moseley "Apartment?"

"Yeah, an apartment building. I've been thinking about this and what you said earlier about the sketches. My theory is that your grandpa and my grandpa were both in some secret society shit and somewhere along the way they both tried to bury it.

And whatever happened in that building, as you saw in the film, was so fucked up.." Moseley catches what he just said in the chapel, pauses, looks up at the figure of Jesus and makes the sign of the cross on his chest. "Forgive me lord." Then continues "..was so fucked up that after nearly 60 plus years my grandfather is still freaked the fuck out. Know what I mean? So much so that he pretty much lit himself on fire. Did you see his face?"

Henry sits back, looks at the address again and starts to build the case in his head on why would he give up? Why now? He's come this far why turn back now? Grandpa might not make it through the night. Would all of this be for nothing? In his hands at this very moment is an exact address to the end of this mystery. The information he needs to create his new book.

Actual facts and surely a treasure trove of more evidence could just be sitting there if he can be the one to find it. For some reason, in the back of Henry's mind, somewhere out there another writer or news agency are already meeting with these Squid people. Just waiting for the right time to break their story. Henry believes that his entire future and glory depends on this story. He's not willing to give up now.

"Alright Mose, but I want to give you $300 so that you can head to Tacoma. Give me your dad's address and I promise that when I write this thing and expose it I'll send you more money."

Moseley interjects "No, seriously Henry. My sister is going to take care of grandpa from here and sell the house. She's giving me money and I already called my dad to give him the news. My plan is to stick around for the next few weeks and make sure gramps is ok. Then, head out to Tacoma by the end of the month. Just in time to spend Halloween with dad."

Henry was so tired that all he could do was smile. They said their goodbyes and Henry wished him well in Washington. For the next hour Henry would sit and stare at the address on the paper. 4802 Bedford Avenue Crown Heights, NY. Below the address there was an arrow pointing down. Nothing else, just down. Henry thought and thought about his promise to Angie. But, things had changed so quickly.

A few hours ago he didn't have this address. She'd understand, right? He's come all this way and now he's holding an actual address to his grandfather's mystery. Lucy would understand. Not Angie, but Lucy would understand. It still didn't help the guilt he felt about not coming home. He was sure that Angie already told Lucy that daddy would be coming home within 24 hours.

Chapter 7 – The keepers

  When Henry first started out this journey the bus ride was very relaxing. Rolling through the east side of Iowa was fun. So many trees and fields. This time, after riding the bus for 12 hours and 3 stops, the bus ride was anything but relaxing. His back and neck hurt and the smell of diesel fumes permeated all of his clothes and jacket. He was sure it was giving him a headache. "Welcome to Brooklyn, NY everyone." The bus driver announced over the speaker. "Before you exit the bus please be sure to have a look around you and make sure you have collected all of your belongings. We sure appreciate you riding with us today and we wish you luck on your adventure. Have a great day. Thank you."

Henry stood up and carefully tossed his backpack over his shoulders without trying to hit any of the other passengers standing around him. This time the bus was packed and he had to wait in line to get off. As soon as he stepped off the bus the air had a different smell. He had heard others say that New York smelled like garbage but he just thought they were pulling his leg. This smell was more like urine he thought. Like the men's restroom at a baseball game. Urine mixed with a light aroma of concrete and someone grilling. He couldn't quite figure it out. Directly in front of him was a large bus map. This is exactly what Henry needed to see how close he was to 4802 Bedford Avenue Crown Heights, NY. With his eyes squinting and fingers scrolling up and down on the board he finally found Bedford Avenue and was please to find that he was only 5 blocks away.

"In that direction" Henry says out loud while pointing West.

While walking Henry was very aware that he wasn't in Iowa anymore. He had never seen so much concrete and walls in his life. Very little trees or grass and no wide open spaces for kids to play. And if there were places for the kids to play it was surrounded by fences. Complete wall to wall steel and concrete. There were so many people and cars out and about that Henry had to check his watch to see what time it was. It was 8:23 at night and the city was bustling it seemed. Back in Sheffield the city would see like a ghost town about now. And it would be much quieter for sure. New Yorker's love their car horns.

After about 20 minutes Henry found Bedford Avenue. He double checked the apartment and house numbers around him to verify which direction on Bedford that he needed to walk. He took a left. Along the way Henry noticed a sign that seemed familiar. It read Prospect Park Subway Station. Henry quickly pulled his backpack off his back and pulled out his grandfather's journal of sketches. After shuffling through the top layer, there it was. Henry pulled out a single sketch from the group and really small in the background there it was. Lightly in pencil behind a group of people his grandfather had sketched a sign that read Prospect Park Subway Station. This was incredible! He thought. His eyes lit up with this discovery. He just had to be close now. Henry shuffled back in the drawings, tossed his backpack over his shoulder and proceeded searching for the 4802 address. Within a few minutes Henry stood in front of a massive apartment building with the address 4802. He was extremely excited to actually be standing on X marks the spot. But, in this case X only marked a general area and not an actual pinpointed spot.

"What the hell now Henry?" He said with a low whisper as to not be heard by the numerous people walking around. Surely they would think he's crazy. After all, Henry had noticed that he might be the only Caucasian in the entire Crown Heights neighborhood. And some of the locals were already giving him odd looks as he passed by. But, Henry didn't mind. He knew his goal was to find out anything he could on the squid people then get back home to write his story.

As Henry approached the building there were several groups of people standing in the courtyard. Reggae music was blaring and some of the men had very thick Haitian accents. He could only pick out a word or two which brought an old friend to mind, Ron. Back in college there was a student he knew named Ron and on the weekends he emceed local talent on the college radio. That guy was so cool. As he continued walking to the front doors he could hear someone every now and then yelling "Hey! Hey mon!" Henry never looked back to even acknowledge the person for fear of striking up a conversation of what he was doing there. It's a free country right? Just some white guy walking into an apartment. No big deal he thought as he comforted himself. As he opened the front doors and stepped inside he could still hear the individual yelling. Henry thought, surely he must have been yelling to someone else. The doors shut hard behind him.

   To Henry's surprise, the apartment building was extremely clean on the inside. Basic, but clean. The entire hallway smelled like lavender cleaning products. Henry kept walking in slowly as to not bring attention to the fact that he had no business being there. A few people passed by him and didn't give him any looks so he began to feel more at ease at the situation. He reached into his coat pocket and pulled out the address and read it out loud "4802 Bedford Avenue. Yup! Here I am." Henry looks back and forth down the long hallway trying to figure out the puzzle. Then, he relooks at the address and looks harder at the arrow pointing down.
"Down? As in, like the basement down grandad?" Henry says with sarcastic tone. "Ok. Let's see if this place has a basement."

Henry walks back to the row of elevators and hits the down button. As he stands there a young woman wearing a white jump suit, white headphones, white sneakers and sunglasses walks up and hits the up button on the elevator. She stands fairly close beside him. Henry was a firm believer in personal space and this teenager didn't seem to follow the same rules as he did. Music was blasting from her headphones and Henry can't help but be concerned for her hearing. The young lady has perfect braids and is smacking on what could be the world's smallest piece of gum ever. But, she's making it snap and pop with every flip in her mouth. It's truly amazing that the gum could even last as long as it has. The elevator slowly arrives with a light ding sound and Henry takes note that the light on the down button has turned off. It looks like this is his ride. He enters the elevator and looks back out at the young lady. He hits B trying not to make eye contact but he notices as the door closes the young woman looks at him over the top of her sunglasses, her gum chewing slowed way down as if she was about to say something. Henry could tell that she knew he didn't know where he was going. Hopefully he could find some more clues in the basement then possibly come back in the morning with a fresh set of eyes. The hard part of finding this place was over. Now it was a hunt for new clues.

The elevator doors open to flickering basement lights. From first glance it doesn't seem like this part of the building gets very many visitors. The paint on the concrete walls are peeling and the floors are extremely dusty. Henry walks forward a bit and stands to take it all in.

He gets a small sinking feeling in his stomach as the elevator door closes and leaves him behind. He's never been afraid of much. When he was little his mother would lift him into the attic to check to see if raccoons had gotten into the rafters. In an odd way this felt similar. Except this time, the raccoon could be a large squid like creature. Or a rat. He laughed to himself.

"Hello?" Henry shouted down the corridor.

For the first time he was actually hoping that nothing answered him back. Henry began walking slowly down the hall. Carefully looking left and right for any signs of a door or hidden room. Unfortunately for Henry he didn't think about packing a flash light. Maybe tomorrow he would stop and purchase one. In the meantime, Henry kept walking and squinting into the darkness.

Some rooms had more lights than others. Some flickered like a haunted house strobe light. For over an hour and a half Henry kept snooping around. On and on and on. From corner to corner he pried on random doors and searched broom closets filled with only cobwebs and dust. Nothing. He couldn't find anything but junk and caged lockers of left behind storage units. Absolutely nothing.

   Taking into consideration that Henry didn't have a place to stay the night, he found a counter and a room with the least amount of rats. He propped up his backpack like a pillow and zipped up his coat. Not even close to the comforts of home, but X marked the spot. After a full day of travelling Henry had no trouble getting comfortable in these surroundings.

His stomach growled and he agreed to himself that tomorrow, while purchasing a flashlight, he'd treat himself to the biggest damn breakfast he's ever had. After all, he's been living on corn chips and pop for the past 4 days. He's found the location. He founded it faster than he thought he would and that absolutely deserves eggs, bacon and pancakes. Heavy on the bacon. Heavy on the pancakes with a side of more pancakes.

The apartment basement is quiet and droplets of water keep a slow steady rhythm. Henry falls fast asleep. There's no sound and the air in the room is still. Henry's dreams are of home and he and Lucy running through the cornfields. Her laughter is contagious and the more she laughs the harder he laughs. They both laugh so hard that they have tears in their eyes.

Henry looks towards the house and notices that Angie is yelling something. He can't hear her over the rustling of the drying corn scratching against his coat. He mouths back "What?" and places his had up to his ear in a cupping shape. Again she yells something. Henry decides that out of respect he needs to hear what her concern is. This time he walks towards Angie and says "What?" This time he can clearly see her face is mad and she yells "WAKE THE FUCK UP!"

Henry quickly realizes that with flashlights in his face 2 to 3 people are all yelling "WAKE THE FUCK UP WHITE BOY!" Each with very think Haitian accents.

A singled out young female voice shouts to his face "Wake up! Grab your shit!"

Henry realizes that it's the young woman from the elevator. She's leading the way while two larger gentlemen are almost lifting Henry off his feet and escorting him back towards the elevators.

"Say, listen." Henry cries out. "I'm sorry for squatting down here but I have no place to go." Nobody says a word as Henry tries to break free from the powerful hands holding his coat.
"If you guys want me to leave, I get it. I'm out of here. Let's just forget it." Henry exclaims.
The young woman no longer wearing headphones, but still working a piece of gum hits the up button on the elevator.

Henry still trying to pull free from the two men says "Seriously, I think you can let.."

The young lady abruptly shuts him down "Shut the fuck up man." And she holds up the journal with all of his grandfather's sketches.

Henry nervously shouts back "No, no, no.. Those are mine. Please be careful. Those were my.."

Again the young woman cuts him off "Your grandfather's?"

In complete amazement Henry stops struggling and looks directly at the young woman. His eyes wide open with awe that she knew what she knew. The elevator opens and the young woman smiles at Henry with a confident smile. One of the men hit the button for 8.

"My name is Phara" the young lady says as she slides the gum to her left cheek. "You're lucky we found you and not someone else. What da fuck you doin' walking around Crown Heights in the middle of da night? Crazy mon!"

Henry looks down at the journal that Phara's holding and softly asks "Could I.. can I get my sketches back please? The mean a lot to.."

"Shit no." Phara interrupts. "You can ask Lovely for them back."

"Lovely?" Henry asks.

"Mom" one of the big guys says.

The elevator doors open and Henry is still being heavily escorted out and down the hall.

"Do you guys mind if I.."

Phara quickly gets into his face and places a finger on his mouth silencing him. They arrive at a door and Henry is man handled in and sat on a couch. The room is extremely colorful. Lots of reds and yellows and numerous candles flicker in the darkness. Henry just realizes that the couch he's sitting on is covered in plastic like his elderly neighbors use to do back in the 80's. He always wondered what good it was having a nice couch if you never actually get to sit on the original fabric?

Phara ducks into a dark room as the two big guys take a seat on either side of him. Nobody says a word and Henry feels very awkward sitting on a complete strangers couch without even a proper introduction. He can hear Phara speaking to someone in the other room but he can't quite make out a single word. Like low mumbling back and forth. Henry also takes note that an old wind-up clock on the mantle says 3:23am. It makes a loud clicking sound that fills the room.

A deep, raspy female voice from the dark room asks "What is your name boy?" It's the same heavy accent as Phara but older, much much older. Henry tries his best to find a shape in the dark door way but it's impossible with the candle light. He half imagines a voodoo looking priestess carrying skulls and wearing snakes to enter the room. Just like in the movies.

"I'm Henry ma'm." Henry responds.

The figure comes forth out of the darkness and slowly enters the room. It's not what he imagined at all. In fact it's an extremely elderly woman wearing a white dress with a long hand woven white shawl. Very proper. Henry can't help but notice that she's wearing a pair of white shoes with 2-inch heels. The shoes are very well cared for and shine even in the low light. It's as though she's already prepared for tomorrow's church service. The woman, using a wooden cane, slowly walks in and takes a seat on the recliner in front of him.

"Well Enry it is den." The woman says as she adjusts her butt in the chair. Every movement she makes is slow and methodical. The men on either side of Henry never make a sound or movement as she enters. Henry can barely even hear them breathing.

"Liking Brooklyn Enry? Like snooping around in people's basements?"

Henry clears his throat and says "Well, actually ma'm, I was just.."

"You two! Leave." Lovely interrupts as she holds up two fingers and points each of them at the men on his sides. Neither of them say a word and promptly exit. It's almost like trained dogs that were just waiting for the command. Now Lovely's two fingers come together and point directly at Henry sitting all alone on the plastic couch.

"Now dat's much bettah, right? All comfy now." Lovely lowers her fingers and readjusts again in her chair. Henry can hear her playing with the dentures in her mouth.

"Phara, can you bring me da TV tray?" Lovely requests.

Phara slides out an old TV tray from behind the chair and unfolds it in front of recliner. Lovely holds out her hand and Phara places the journal on the tray in front of her. He's completely uncomfortable seeing his grandfather's journal in in front of Lovely. What will she think? What does she know about them?

"Let me be blunt Enry." Lovely says.

"Who else knows about dis? And don't lie to me." She says as she looks over the sketches. "I have a gift for tellin' when a man be lyin'. More like a curse actually Enry. No?"

Henry keeps his eyes on the journal and plays stupid "Who knows what Miss Lovely? I found those sketches a few days ago at a garage sale actually. I found a few old comics book as well. Vintage! And, they had one of those.." Henry raises his hands and makes a swirling motion. "One of those old wooden things that when you place a marble at the top, the little gear wheels keep turning, and the marble goes like.."

"I can tell it's gonna be a long night Enry." Lovely says loudly as she looks up with her piercing dark eyes and looks directly at Henry. "Who.. Else.. Knows?" She asks again pausing with each word making sure Henry understands the question..

Henry sits back in the couch a bit and thinks hard on the question. Obviously Moseley knows and so does his wife and Lucy. But he's not about to mention their names or sell out Moseley. He's already put them all through so much. And he's not even sure what would happen here? Would Lovely send out some sort of Haitian hit squad? To little Sheffield, Iowa? And for what? Some sketches of a squid thingy? An art student could have drawn those. Naturally he's seen the films and the horror of the man dissecting it in front of an audience, but. What does it matter to Lovely? Why is she so interested? What does she know? Henry is determined to protect his family, so he twists his story and says.

"One guy knows. An old guy I met in Cleveland. But, he was terribly burnt and I'm not even certain he's alive anymore. You can look it up in the news. I'd like to know if he made It myself actually."

Lovely looks back down at the sketches and takes in a deep breath.

"One.. Guy? Are you sure you weren't jibber jabbing with anyone else around the neighborhood about squid creatures?" Lovely asks.

Henry takes in a big breath and says "Actually, I just arrived late this evening and came straight here from the bus stop. I'm writing a story. A book. I think these squid creatures would be an incredible story to share. I mean, can you imagine how huge this story would be to the world if they exist? Can I get a glass of water please?"

Lovely simply raises her hand and Phara quickly returns with a clear glass of water.
Henry takes a sip and continues "I mean, we're talking about the find of the century. What do you know about them? Are they here? In this building?"

"HHhhmmm, interesting Enry." Lovely smiles and says as she cracks a smile. "I like you. You's a honest mon. It's contagious. Lemme guess, Wisconsin? Minnesota?"

Henry laughs, "Iowa ma'm. Corn." Lovely smiles like a Cheshire cat.

"Well, you in luck Enry. They do exist." Lovely says with a whisper.

Henry leans up on the couch in excitement "They do?"

"Yes Enry, dey is very real. But are you willin to make da right choice dis night?" Lovely closes the journal and sits back in her chair.

"Da way I sees it you's got two paths to choose from here, now, tonight! Dis very moment. Then I need to get my beauty rest. Long day tomorrow. Long day. De first path is that you go ahead and get some rest on dat very couch and at the crack of dawn you pack up, grab a muffin and go home. Never to speak about dis day again or foolishness about squid people evah! Dey'll nevah believe you anyway Enry. I'd even pay for your ticket back home. Forget this place Enry. Forget the squids. Do you have a family Henry? I don't see any wedding ring."

Henry looks down at his finger and gladly remembers that he hasn't worn it in years. Not because of the problems he's been having with Angie, only because his dog Mr. Nibbles almost lost a tooth while playing. "No ma'm. I don't have a family." Henry replies.

Lovely continues "Enry, I gets da feeling that you're not the kind of mon who can't just let things go. It's my curse remembah? I knows dat you don't like da first path without even knowin' the second path. So let me explain." Lovely slides the journal to the side and looks directly at Henry "Jus like da first path you can go ahead and sleep here tonight, be sure to grab a muffin in the morning. The difference.. If you want to continue dis adventure and meet a real life squid-man face-to-face.." Henry's eyes widen. "It'll be costing you $5,000 cash. Or a travelers check, up to you. Just remember that when this thing is over and you've met the squid-man. I wonder if you think it will be worth it? Will it fill that empty hole in your heart Enry?"

Henry looks stunned at this request. There's no possible way that he can scrounge up $5 let alone $5,000.

His eyes start to blink rapidly as he processes the options he's just been given. He's come so far, and by all the evidence it's here. Somewhere in this building. It's here. A squid-man no less. If he can meet him, snap off a photo with his camera. Boom! He can head home, write his story and live out the rest of his life on the royalties. Maybe even a documentary or better yet a TV series.

"Enry?" Lovely asks.

Without hesitation Henry replies "Second path! But, I'll need a day to figure out how to get $5,000. I'm broke and I don't know anybody holding onto that kinda cash." Henry notices Phara's head drop down a bit. As if disappointed at his decision.

"Fair enough Enry my boy, get some rest. You have until tomorrow evening to get the cash. While you out tomorrow you'll need to grab a couple more tings" Lovely says as she scooches forward in the chair in an attempt to stand.

Phara grabs her by the arm and helps her to her feet. Lovely continues "You gonna to need a water-proof flashlight and a garbage bag. Tomorrow night, once we have da money, my grandson Edgard will take you, and only you, into da secret chamber and introduce you to the squid-man. During the day you will say nothing to nobody about this." Lovely stops in her door way. "Do you understand this Enry? Nobody? If you so much as breathe a word about da squid you won't have a story to write." Lovely looks back at Henry and continues "And you won't have a hand to write with. Clear Enry?"

"I got it." Henry replies.

Lovely doesn't say another word and disappears into the darkness of her room again.

Chapter 8 – The Deep Dark

By the time Henry woke up there was nobody in the apartment. He shyly peeked into Lovely's room and found it odd that there was nothing in it, just a single chair in the middle of the room. Did she pull a magic trick and disappear? Not even a closet or a window. Just a square room with white walls. Suddenly Henry's forehead got warm as he remembered that his mission today was to somehow scrounge up $5,000. How the hell does a man with no job, no credit pull up $5,000? He sure as hell couldn't ask Angie for money that he knows they don't have. There's no time to call up the bank and take out a loan using the house as collateral. And Again, Angie would kill him.

Then it came to him. A cunning idea came to Henry. Not a good idea. But a despicable plan that Henry thought might just work. He thought maybe he could call up the pastor and pull a fast one. Who else had money that he could borrow? He knew for a fact that the pastor had money. His mom's money! The family money! As a matter of fact it should have been his money. Henry started to recall all the times that he would stop by to see his mom on the farm and for some odd reason, wouldn't you know it, the pastor was there. Always lurking in the background. Why was he always there? This was him mom. His farm. Henry also recalled the afternoon when his mom gave him the news that she was leaving everything to the church. The pastor was there! Henry remembers that it was the pastor that walked him to his truck, talking about how he feared that his mother had lost her mind. But she didn't did she? No. It was all an evil scam to swindle his mom. To swindle him. No, Henry wasn't going to let him get away with it. This plan was more like revenge.

Henry thought some more. He couldn't just call him up and ask for a flat out loan. The plan had to be meticulously thought out enough that the pastor would be 100% compelled to wire the money within the next few hours. Once, when Henry was the editor of the Mason City Globe Gazette, he recalled a story about a woman hustling her husband out of $75,000 dollars by claiming she was kidnapped. The foolish husband at the time thinking that his wife was in danger took out all of their savings and wired it directly to one of those check cashing places you see on every corner. It wasn't long before detectives learned that she was actually in Las Vegas with her new boyfriend. Spending that $75,000 on booze, gambling and sex toys. Good story that always made Henry smile.

Henry looks around for a phone and a phone book. In the back of his head he's already rehearsing his lines and he practices out loud.

"Oh god, Pastor? Please! I need your help." Henry even pauses for the part where the pastor should be asking what's wrong?

"Pastor.. Tom." That's good Henry thinks, let's use his real name.

"Tom, I've been kidnapped and I have a gun to my head. They say that if I don't get.." Henry stops to rethink the amount he should ask for considering how much the pastor has stolen from him. "They say if I don't get $10,000 dollars by 3:00pm they're going to kill me. Please Tom! Please!!!!" That sounded great Henry thought. Maybe he might need to put a lot more desperation into his voice once he's actually on the phone and whip up some tears. But, not bad for a beginner.

Just like that and according to plan Henry got ahold of the Pastor. And sure enough he was very willing to help Henry out in this time of need. The pastor spoke of Angie and Lucy and even the police. Henry kindly asked the pastor to just keep this between them. He was fairly confident that these guys meant business but they weren't going to really hurt him as long as he got the money.

By noon, Henry picked up the money at a local check cashing place that was only 4 blocks away. A quick easy walk that also passed by a hardware store. Two birds with one stone Henry thought. He found a wide selection of water-proof flash lights and a box of black garbage sacks. Once Henry had the money he made his way back towards the apartment building.

Walking around with $10,000 in the middle of Brooklyn made him extremely uncomfortable. As he was walking he spotted an old pay phone booth and he thought about Lucy. What would it hurt now just to give her a call. After all, if all goes well he'll be coming home within the day by plane. With the extra $5,000 he couldn't wait to fly home first-class and wash his hands with one of those hot rags they hand out with tongs. Sip some champagne even. Celebrate a bit on what he's about to experience this evening. He's within a few hours he'll have what could be the story of the century. Real life, living and breathing squid people.

Henry steps up to the phone booth, lifts the phone off the receiver and grabs a handful full of quarters out of his bag. He places the quarters in a pile on top of the phone and calls Lucy's school.

"Hello, Mrs. Nelson? Yeah, it's Henry, Lucy's dad. I know this seems kinda odd but I've been out of town for the past week and if you don't mind I'd just love a 5 minute chat with Lucy, ok? Can you grab her for me?" Henry switches ears with the phone so that he can get a better look out towards the street.

Suddenly you can hear a tiny little voice on the other end. Henry's face lights up like magic. His eyes get a bit glossy.

"Hello? Sweetie? Is that you baby girl?" Henry says with a grin from ear to ear.
On the other end Lucy is just as excited to be taking a special call from her daddy during the middle of a school day.

"Hello daddy. When are you coming home?"

"Soon, very very soon. I'm in New York! I made it!" Henry adds. "I've got to finish up that book I was telling you about then I'll be on a plane home, ok?"

"Ok" Lucy replies with the tiniest of voices. "Mr. Nibbles misses you too daddy."

"I bet he does baby girl. Tell you what. You better get back to class now ok. Just keep looking up in the sky tomorrow and I might be in one of those big planes we see all the time, I'll be waving down, ok?"

Lucy laughs "Ok daddy. I'll be waving back. When you get home let me know if you could see me waiving back ok?"

"Ok sweetie. Hey, I love you more than anything. Understand?" He says as his voice cracks a bit. "You're my everything."

"I love you too daddy. Very much. Mrs. Nelson says I need to get back to class now. I'll be waving." Lucy says as the phone hangs up.

Over the next few hours Henry does his best to keep a low profile. He finds a great little Korean BBQ restaurant and splurges a bit. He even orders up a martini. He can't recall the last time he had such an expensive drink. He continues walking back towards the apartment. His mind racing with excitement at what tonight's adventure will bring. He's even a bit nervous. What do you even say to a squid-man? Do they even speak? How do the Haitians even arrange such a meeting in the first place? What's the flash light for? What's the garbage bag for? Where will they meet? Will the squid-man just come to the apartment? So many questions keep spinning around in Henry's head. So many details he will have to pay attention to in order to capture this event. How will it end? Will they simply give a big hug and "say nice to meet you" then be on their way?

Henry's head was spinning with the same questions over and over all the way back up to Lovely's apartment. The door was open so he just made himself at home again on the plastic couch. This time he brought along a few snacks for the few hours remaining until night. Before anyone came back to the apartment he made sure to count out exactly $5,000 so that nobody else would know he had more than that. Just in case this was all just one big scheme to rob him he hid the money in a back panel in his backpack.

With his mind going round and round a few hours seemed like forever. He checked his watch repeatedly. He smiled thinking back on his conversation he had with Lucy. He had only been gone a few days and already it seemed like she sounded older and more mature. He wondered if Lucy would tell Angie that she spoke to him that day? In a weird way it made Henry feel good knowing that Angie would find out and in some way feel jealous that he only called to speak with Lucy. Henry smiled at this small little dig.

Chapter 9 – Still waters

All of Henry's life he always felt as though he wasn't in control. It was never up to him. He felt as though he had to sit back and just abide by whatever was given to him. It was never his plans or his goals but theirs. The Globe Gazette, Angie, mom and dad, the Pastor, the neighbor kid that always commented on his clothes. All of them. Heck, even Mr. Nibbles wasn't the dog he wanted but his mother-in-law insisted on that specific breed. Why would it even matter to her? She doesn't have to live with it. Now tonight, within the hour, this was Henry's time. It was his time to take charge for once and grab the reigns. From now on Henry would be his own man and reinvent himself. He felt good with this new him. He felt empowered and ready to take on the world.

Just then the door begins to open. In walks in an overly exuberant skinny man with the whitest brightest teeth that Henry has ever seen. Henry stands up from the couch to greet him. The very dark-skinned Haitian is wearing a colorful beanie cap, military green cargo pants, black t-shirt and a military looking vest. At first Henry isn't quite sure what to make of this character but his smile is making him smile. Before Henry can say anything the man joyfully yells out "You must be da Enry mon, ya?!"

Before Henry can even reply the skinny guy comes in and puts Henry into a huge bear hug and giggles the entire time. As though Henry is a long lost relative or something.

"Yes, I'm Henry. And you must be.."

"Easy Eddie ma name!" Edgard interrupts. "Now I don't wanna be no buzz kill on this magic of magical days, but do ya have da five thousand dollahs momma Lovely requested?"

Henry reaches into his pocket and grabs the rolled up cash and hands it over to Eddie. Now that he's been greeted, Henry also notices that 2 other gentlemen have entered the room. Not the same guys from last night but two new big guys in similar military apparel as Edgard. They both politely smile as Henry looks at each of their faces.

"Phara's not coming with us?" Henry asks while looking towards the door as if expecting her to walk in any second.

"Oh no, not today brudah. She gets squirmy wit da squidy if you know what I mean." Edgard looks back at the two men and they all laugh in unison. Henry can't help but join in with a nervous laugh as well. For a second, Henry even imagined what it would be like to invite Eddie back home to little Sheffield, Iowa.

Can you imagine it? Eddie was the most charismatic man he's ever met. Most colorful. He toyed with the idea of introducing this guy to his very stuffy mother-in-law. Henry smiles at this idea. It would be worth it he the price of admission just to watch her squirm.

Eddie is counting the money on the kitchen counter "$4,700, $4,800, $4,900.. " He stops and looks at Henry with a very serious face. "Enry.. Enry, Enry, Enry." Henry's day dream smile slowly fades as he can see that there's something wrong with Eddie's count in the money. To be honest, he hadn't even been listening to what the total was as Eddie stopped.

"Enry. Momma Lovely said $5,000. Eddie says with a stone cold face glaring at Henry. With Money in hand Eddie begins slowly walking towards Henry. Just like a cat does when it's stalking it's prey.

Henry takes a big throaty gulp as Eddie gets closer and closer. What went wrong he wonders? Did he miss a certain amount. Will he be forced to open his back pack and expose his secret hiding place with the remaining $4,800 plus change?

As the color runs from Henry's face he asks "Momma Lovely said $5,000 and I thought that's what I handed you. I apologize if the amount.. isn't.. correct."

Now Eddie is standing nose to nose with Henry. With wide eyes they both stare into one another eyes. Henry can even smell that at some point Eddie has been smoking a cigarette. The smell isn't coming off of Eddie's clothes, it's for sure his breath. That's how close they are.

Eddie breaks the tension with a huge grin and starts laughing. "Did you see that brudahs? Ha ha ha! Did I get him?" In between their two faces Eddie holds up a $100 bill. "You over counted you knuckle head. Ha ha ha!"

Henry slowly lifts his hand to receive the $100 and joins Eddie in laughter. How the heck did that happen? In all of his excitement did he accidentally dropped in another $100 dollar bill. To be honest, that's the first time Henry has ever held that much money in the first place. Completely honest mistake. But the look on Eddie's face was terrifying. He may have been fun and games on the outside but wow, he certainly had a darker side and Henry hoped to never see that side again. Either that or Eddie should be using that money and become an actor. It was truly a tense moment.

"Alright Enry, grab your bag and let's head to the deep down." Eddie says as he waves his hand at the two others at the door. They all file out of the small apartment and head towards the elevator in a small pack.

The bigger of the two men hits the down button and they wait. You can hear the elevator motor kick in and there's a small whistle sound pushing through the crack in the elevator doors. Henry was still replaying Eddie's acting scene in the back of his head. It actually made Henry feel more comforted that Eddie returned the overage on the money. In most instances even an honest man would be tested to just pocket the extra $100 and never say a word. The doors open and the men file in. Eddie presses B and the doors close.

"One more ting Enry.. Almost slipped my mind. You got the da flashlight? Garbage bag?" Eddie asks.

Henry quickly opens his back pack and allows Eddie to look inside the main compartment. There sits and entire box of 30 garbage bags. He reaches in and pulls out the flashlight like a kid on his first day of school Henry shows off his new toy "Water proof." He says with a please expression.

   "Good job bouy." Eddie says as he pats Henry on the back.

   The elevator doors open and the men file out and walk down the hall. This feels good to Henry since he has already inspected most of this area. It was familiar and not spooky in the slightest. The small group continues walking down the hall and they take a hard left to a room full of locker cages. The room is very dark and has at least 30 plus storage cages.

Some are open and some are locked and stuffed with furniture and odds and ends. They all stop in the back corner in front of a locked cage. Eddie fumbles with some keys and unlocks the cage door. One of the men politely pushes Henry back a bit as to make room for the two men to enter the storage unit first. Henry stands and watches as the men lift up a couch and move it to the side. Then they grab 3 or 4 bicycles and place those on top of the couch. For the next 8 minutes or so, the men painstakingly move one item after another. Each item is cared for and not mishandled. Henry realizes that they're uncovering something that's been hiding underneath the junk. No wonder he couldn't find anything last night. Unless you knew it was there, nobody would even bother to look.

   Eddie hands Henry a large flashlight and gestures a finger towards the middle of the floor "Enry, point it here." He asks.

Henry aims the light in the general direction that Eddie pointed. But there's nothing there except a large vintage burgundy rug. As the two men grab an end and peel it back, it exposes two large metal double doors flush to the ground. Henry keeps his light fixed in that spot as they completely move the rug aside.

"You see Enry?" Eddie says as he reaches back for the light that Henry is holding. "Big doors for a big boogey man." Eddie smiles.

The two men mean lean over and pull up metal rings on the top overlapping door. There's a large creaking metal on metal sound as they swing the door up. So loud that it reverberates down the hall and echoes a bit. Once peeled back Eddie points the flashlight into the hole.

Henry careens his neck a bit as if expecting bats or the squid-man to be just on the other side looking back. But as Henry looks closer into the hole, the light exposes only a few top steps dropping down and into darkness.

Eddie shines the light in Henry's face and says "You go first."

As Henry shields his eyes from the blinding light he tries to gage whether or not Eddie is being serious or not. He takes a step closer to the dark opening in the ground and pulls out his own flashlight. He can smell the dampness and there's a hallow sound of emptiness coming back out. It reminded him of the old wells his parents had on their farm. Except for those he could see the bottom.

"What dangers await us in the deep dark Enry?" Eddie asks with a wild-eyed look on his face.

Henry takes a step closer to the hole trying to figure out how exactly to step in without tumbling all the way down. It's so dark and his eyes can't quite see where the first step begins. He knows it has to be just within the door. Just then Eddie grabs him by the coat and laughs. He gestures towards one of the men with a wave of his neck and the man quickly hops in the hole. As Henry looks on in amazement, a light quickly flicks on from within. Henry peeks in further and can now clearly see a more steps. Beyond the metal doors is a large hidden cylinder shaped chamber. The metal steps hug the walls and continue to go down as far as Henry can see. Lights are wrapped around the metal steps and as far as Henry can tell they keep going down hundreds of feet.

One by one each man follows the next into the chamber. Henry watches as one of the men stops to shut the large metal door behind them. It makes a loud clang as it slams home. Henry leans over the railing a bit and listens below as if trying to understand just how deep the pit goes. Nothing bounces back. The vibration keeps echoing down and down.

"C'mon" Eddie says as he begins walking down the steps.

Step by step the men go round and around down the large tube. Only the sound of their feet makes sounds and every so often a rusty step or two squeaks as they pass by. The railing seems sturdy enough and every so often Henry points his $8 flashlight down to the bottom as if expecting to see some sort of bottom. And yet, nothing but darkness.

The men continued to march and the sounds of their steps began to sound like a rhythm to Henry. It was melodic. As they marched, Henry's anticipation grew. In his mind he kept detailed notes about the experience. Right down to the rusty railings and the brick pattern in the chamber. Someone had to place every single one of these bricks, it had to have 50 taken years he thought. Was this the place that his grandfather had been? Did his grandfather take part in the construction of this room? Where will it end? Will the squid-man just be sitting in a lounge chair at the very bottom? Smoking a pipe and watching reruns with a bag of chips? Henry smiled at the image of this. One of the men makes a clicking sound with his tongue and Henry watches as Eddie points his flash light over the edge of the railing. Henry looks over the edge as well and can finally see ground. He looks back at his watch and realizes that they have been walking tirelessly for over an hour and 20 minutes. That was the longest stair case Henry has ever been on. He glances back up in amazement of how well preserved the chamber actually is considering the years it's been hiding down here. Finally, he thinks.

Henry asks "Is this it Eddie?"

"No mon." Eddie replies back with a laugh. "We're only half way. To da bottom. You want the good news or the bad news Enry?"

Henry stops for a second to catch his breath. "I've always liked the bad news first but I'm changing my mind today Eddie. What's the good news?"

Eddie reaches the bottom and walks out onto a solid dirt covered floor. As he walks towards the opposite side of the chamber he says "The good news.." Somewhere in the darkness you can hear Eddie opening what sounds like a metal box. "The good news.. is.." With a loud heavy clunk sound lights flood the entire area where they stand. Henry smiles with pleasure at the feel of the warm lights on his face.

"The good news is that we won't be walking from here." Eddie says with a smile as he gestures at what appears to be a large freight elevator shaft on the wall behind him.

"The bad news is that we still have a long ride to get to the bottom." The worse news.. when it's time to go home Enry. We still have to walk all da way back up dem steps. Do you feel bad for me Enry? And you know it's easier going down then up." Henry hadn't thought of that. He's been so excited about meeting the squid-man that it completely slipped his mind about the trip back up. It will be a long walk back up to the top.

"Hey Enry." Eddie says holding open his jacket and showing off his physique. "Now you know why I'm so damn skinny! Ha ha ha!!" Everyone laughs as Eddie opens the gates on the freight elevator.

As they enter the elevator and start to travel down it dawns on Henry that if he's going to capitalize on this experience why not throw some question and answers at Eddie. After all, they must have been guarding this place for years. Which means that one his elders must have been involved in some way, right? Was it Lovely? Her family. So many questions.

Henry sits down on the elevator floor and opens his back pack. "Eddie, would you mind if I took some notes and asked you a few questions?"

Eddie laughs and says "Sure mon. Ask me anything you like. We got time."

Henry gets comfortable on the floor, flips open the first page of a brand new notebook. Scribbles his pen on the top to ensure it works and begins with his questions.

"Alright, so how long have you been the keepers of the squid people?"

Eddie lights up a cigarette and softly says "Next question."

Henry looks up at Eddie with an unexpected look on his face. "Ok, how did you find the squid people? Was Lovely involved in the beginning?"

Eddie passes the cigarette to one of the men and replies "Next question."

Again, Henry looks up at Eddie with an unexpected look on his face. "How many more people have you brought down here to meet the Squid-man?"

Eddie exhales a puff of smoke with a reply of "Next question."

Quickly Henry feels that he's being made the butt of a joke. Even the two other men have been chuckling at his expense. Henry thinks long and hard about his next question.

There has to be a question that will force Eddie to give up some sort of dirt. How can he prove to Eddie that he's not just a tourist. That he's got a vested interest in the history of the squid people. That he means to do right by them. Obviously these keepers don't want their secret to get out so they can't say much. But, maybe the right question will crack the safe on Eddie and a speck of details will spill out. And just like that, it comes to Henry. The footage that he witnessed at Moseley's house that day. That man was just hacking away at the creature like a side of beef. And his mother, what was it that she said? "We ate them.." That's right! "She said we ate them." This time Henry stood up for this next question. He wanted to look deep into the eyes of Eddie for this one.

"Can you tell me why people ate them?"

"Gwo dyòl!!" The men shout out as they lunge at Henry. Eddie pushes them back and yells "Enbesil, don't know no bettah! He dumb."

"Listen Enry." Eddie says as he slides Henry into a corner.

"Listen, listen. Trow away what you know and what you tink you know Enry. Those were dark days for the squid people. Very dark." Eddie stops, takes a step back and stares at Henry who's still a bit shaken up by the immediate reaction he got.

"Yes, it's true Enry. People ate them." Eddie says with a saddened face.

"People are naturally violent Enry. Name one time in the civilized world when the civilized remained civilized. Huh? No Enry.. We are a planet of animals. No matter how educated you are or how many degrees you collect from da school you still an animal. Deep down."

Eddie pauses and reaches his hand behind him as if signaling that he needs another puff of the cigarette. One of them lights up a new one and hands it to Eddie. This gave Henry a chance to reflect on what was just said. It is extremely disturbing to think that his grandparents could have taken part in such a thing. What drove them to that? Was it some sort of cult? Why was the military involved? Did they know this was going on? No wonder his mother had that terrified look on her face in her last days. She would have only been a child and witnessing that horror. Suddenly Henry felt differently about his grandfather. How could he do that to his daughter? Henry's thoughts went back to when his grandfather use to give him rides on the old tractor. And the times when he would take him out in the middle of the night and just sit in the flat bed of a pickup truck looking up at the stars. Those were great memories that he had always held dear. Now they've been corrupted.

Abruptly Henry imaged if it were Lucy and the repulsion of forcing her to eat pieces and parts of a squid like man. The dread that Henry felt was awful. Did his grandfather make his mom watch while they hacked away at it? Did she hear the same shrieks that he had heard in Moseley's basement? My god it's astonishing that his mother could even function at all through the years with those memories.

"You ok Enry?" Eddie asks. "You look as though you gonna be sea sick." The men chuckle again as Henry can hear the elevator slowing down.

Chapter 9 – The invite

Finally, the elevator reaches the bottom with a soft landing. Henry was thinking that Eddie was right about is sea sick comment. He does feel sick to his stomach a bit. Understandably, thinking about his family eating defenseless squid people would be unnerving for anyone. No wonder Moseley's grandpa was off-tilt as well. If he truly was the camera man, he had to bear witness to the atrocities and collect a military paycheck. How would you move on from that? What happened to all of the other men in those films? Did they all lose their minds at some point as well? Like his mother did?

Eddie pulls open the large elevator cage doors with both hands.

"Now here's what you need to know Enry. Day don't speak words like we do. They make clicking sounds. The good news for us is dat we have narrowed down the clicking sounds to a basic way to communicate wit dem. Cool? One click means yes. Two clicks means no. Easy peasy. Got it?"

Henry nods his head and repeats what he just learned "One click yes. Two clicks no. Got it." Henry lifts his small flashlight and aims it around the room. It's not as powerful as Eddie's flashlight but he can make out that he appears to be in a very large room, like a warehouse, with rows and rows of pillars. The air is heavy with the smell of salt water. Henry recalled that smell from when he was little and his parents had once taken to him to California on vacation.

Eddie walks up beside him and shines the light further into the room. Henry can now see that the room is sloped downward a bit. Half of the room is filled with water. The half that they're standing on is dry brown dirt.

"Whatchu think?" Eddie asks.

Henry doesn't know what to say at this moment. This has always been the goal and now here he is preparing to meet the thing that haunted his mother in the end. The thing that his grandfather had spent hours sketching. The reason he left his family behind. Here it was. He was getting that nervous feeling again in his stomach. Within a few short minutes he'd be face-to-face with an undiscovered creature.

Eddie asks "No? Nothing now? Isn't this what you wanted?"

"Absolutely. I just.. You don't know how far I've come to be here. What I've sacrificed for this moment. Thank you." Henry says.

"Oh no mon. Don't tank me. Stay here and I'll signal dat you're ready." Eddie walks away from Henry and towards the water. With his weaker flashlight Henry can see Eddie walk to the water's edge and give out two large whistles.

"Is that it?" Henry asks. "Is that the signal?"

Eddie quickly walks back towards Henry with a hurried look on his face. "Ok, here we go. Couple tings. You got the garbage bag?"

Henry drops his backpack and replies "yeah, right here."

Eddie grabs the bag from Henry and jerks it up and down trying to fluff it open. "Ok, take off all of your clothes and put dem in da bag. Quickly!"

Henry looks at him stunned "What?" He says

"Quickly! Take dem off now and place them in the bag. You wanted to meet squid people, right?! Now in da bag."

Stupefied Henry does as commanded fast as he can. The jacket and shirt came off easy. As he sits on the ground to take his pants off he can see that the look on the men's faces is of apprehension. One of the men even has his hand under his shirt as if he has a weapon on standby. What would make them so afraid? Why would they even allow this to happen if they believe that the creature is dangerous?

"Quickly! Now!" Eddie shouts.

Henry slams all of his clothes into the bag. He even uses Eddie's shoulder to steady himself as he pulls off each sock and throws them in. As soon as the socks are in Eddie spins the bag and ties the top. Henry standing there astonished watches as the 3 men back into the elevator and close the doors behind.

"WAIT!? WHAT!?" Henry screams as he races to try and pry the doors back open.

"Don't worry Enry! Everything going to be alright! Squid people Enry. You wanted to meet squid people!" Eddie yells out as the elevator starts to go back up.

Henry clinging on the elevator doors yells up "Fuck this! No! Don't leave me you assholes!" For the next few minutes he continued to yell back up the elevator shaft. Every now and then he could hear Eddie shouting something back down. But, he couldn't make it out over the elevator clanging back and forth. What the hell was this he thought? What was once excitement had rapidly turned to fear. Would they come back down and pick him up eventually? Could he recall the elevator himself and go back up? Henry's heart was racing and thoughts flew by a hundred miles an hour. He's never felt so trapped in his life.

The only light he had now was coming from his poorly made water-proof flashlight laying on the ground. Backpack? He dropped to his hands and knees and dug around for his backpack. Did they take that as well. Henry shouted out "Shit! Shit, shit, shit." Everything he owned was in there. The laptop, the money. Henry yelled out in aggravation "You gotta be kidding me!!"

Just then Henry heard the water move behind him. It made the hair on the back of his neck stand on end. He hustled to grab the flashlight and pointed it out towards the water. His eyes squinted as he waived it back and forth. Panicking Henry quickly got to his feet.

"Hello?" He shouted in over the water. No sound.

He noticed a ripple coming from behind a pillar so he quickly aimed his flashlight in that direction fighting for a glimpse of what was moving.

"Hello?" Henry asked.

This time he heard a deep wet "Flabbabooosh" sound coming from behind another pillar to his left. His eyes peered hard through the dim light. Now he knew for a fact that he wasn't alone in the room. That was the sound of something breathing in the water for sure. Like when a whale comes up for a breath. But this sounded more like a wet flapping exhale. Henry slowly panned the flashlight back and forth over the water. Whatever it is he didn't want to scare it with the light flailing about. Just then Henry notices something sticking up from the water. It almost looks like a wet paper bag floating on the surface. Henry cautiously moves towards the shape, being extra careful as to not get too close to the water. He blinks his drying eyes in the hopes they'll refocus on the shape. He pushes his small flashlight further towards the water. That's when he sees it. This whole time he was pushing to get a glimpse of the shape and that entire time the shape has eyes and is looking directly at Henry. The revelation startles him and he falls backwards.

"Oh shit, hello?" Henry says towards the shape.

Again he hears the sound of "Flabbabooosh." But this time he sees the bubbles coming up from under the creatures face. It begins to glide towards him and Henry scurries on his butt back towards the wall. Never allowing the creature to escape the minimal light that he has aimed at it. Henry looks in astonishment as the squid creature continues moving towards the shore line. Up and up, more and more of it reveals itself to Henry's. It's exactly as his grandfather had sketched. A long upper squid-like body with tentacles dripping over its bony knees. It even had feet. It didn't have toes but those were certainly feet. The creature, now on dry land, stands and stares at Henry. Every now and then it's large docile looking eyes would blink. As Henry, mouth wide open, frozen stared back.

"Click." A sound came from the squid-man.

Henry, closing his mouth remembered what Eddie had said about the clicks. One click for yes and two for no.

"Ha-hello, my name is Henry." Henry winced at his comment. Thousands of years of evolution stands in front of him and all he can think of to say was that?

He tries again. "I've come a long way to meet you. I'd love to know more about you and your kind.."

The squid-man gives off a single "click."

Henry thinks, good. This is progress. This is truly remarkable what's happening here. Two beings separated by time, living on the same planet are actually holding a conversation. This is amazing. What's the next question he wonders.

"Do you live in this room?"

"Click. Click." Comes from the creature.

"Huh!" Henry says as he thinks of another angle "Is your home underneath this room further down?"

The squid-man makes a single "click."

Now Henry's beyond intrigued at this. All of this could be just a front? The tip of the iceberg! Possibly, below his feet there's an entire squid city loaded with millions and millions of squid people. Squid kids! Squid teens and moms and dads? An entire community just waiting to be discovered. Why didn't the Haitians capitalize on this more? Eddie seems like a money-making kinda guy. Why pass this up? This would be the biggest discovery in the entire history of man. Books would be written. Bonds would be built with their leaders and our leaders. Political systems aligning to work together for the planet.

Henry stands up and brushes off the dirt from his butt. "Would it be possible for me to see your home?"

Without hesitation Henry is given his answer with a single "Click."

Henry's expression says it all. This is it. What good would it have been just to have met a squid person. Now, he has the chance to meet the entire community. When he gets back he'll have more than enough to write about. He'll make those idiots at the Gazette regret the day he walked out the door. This story was a guaranteed Pulitzer Prize. He wondered how many talk shows he would be on, each asking deep questions about the squid people and of course he would be the only authority on the matter. But then Henry realized. His excitement level came way down when he realized that squid world was under water. Obviously he hadn't adapted to breathing water like his squid friend standing there has adapted to air. Henry knew he'd have to break the news to his new friend.

"Hey, uh. I'd love to come visit your home but.. I can't hold my breath very long and I kinda sucked in swim class."

The squid-man just stood there and stared back at Henry. Suddenly he noticed something moving. A long pale, skinny finger comes out from under the tentacles and points towards the wall behind Henry. Henry can't help but keep looking at the hand. He didn't expect that at all. That was something he never saw in his grandpa's drawings. He didn't even see that in the films. Now, there it was. A man-like hand pointing. Henry turns his head to see what the creature is pointing to. Along the back wall in the darkness there's a grouping of items huddled there.

Henry shines his light and starts walking closer. He can't quite make out the shape with his crappy flashlight but then he sees it. He turns and looks back at the creature with a large grin. Now, he's never been scuba diving in his life but there it all is. A single tank, one of those breathing valves and a mask.

"Buddy!" Henry calls out.

Henry quickly straps on the gear the best he knows how. Places the mouth piece in his mouth and turns the dial on the top of the tank clockwise. He hears air tighten up the hose-line so it must be working. He takes a couple puffs to test it and sure enough air is flowing. Henry picks up his flashlight and walks back towards the squid-man.

"All set I hope." Henry says as he pulls down the mask over his face.

The creature makes a single "click."

Once again, there it is. The squid reaches out his clammy looking hand towards Henry. Henry looks down at the hand and back into the large eyes of the squid-man. He hadn't planned on this part and the hand looked like a dead fish. And every now and then a tentacle would loop around a finger. It was disgusting. But the discomfort would be well worth the reward.

Henry reaches out and takes hold of the creature's hand. Cold and clammy just as expected. The two move towards the water and before you know it they submerge. Henry is doing his best to hang onto the squid-man's hand with one hand and the flashlight in the other. Once in the water Henry gets the feeling that they are moving father fast in the water. The squid-man may not look like much on the surface, but below water he was powerful.

They're moving so rapidly that Henry can never get a ling enough glimpse at his surroundings. He definitely saw the large crack as they passed through, but the water is so dark he can't see much else. It's a deep dark greenish blue void. Bit by bit walls and caverns pass by Henry's light. They are moving so fast that he has no choice but to stop trying to look for shapes and things in the darkness.   But to just sit back and let the light hopefully define something along the way.

Instantly, right before his face another squid person is swimming beside them. Henry is thrilled! Then another. And another. Henry aims his light around and realizes that he's surrounded by at least 12 other squid people. They are all moving and around Henry as if to get a better look at the human.

This is exactly what Henry set out to do. He's done it! He's made contact. While there's a million idiots on the surface looking for aliens from space. Here's Henry, dancing with them right under our feet.

Henry feels a quick jerking motion. The squid creature seems to be getting jealous of all of the attention he's getting. Henry's stomach drops as he feels he's dipping in and out of caverns now. He never gets a solid look but he's sure he's in the heart of squid city now. The passage ways are getting tighter and tighter as he floats by. His flashlight is only seeing brown potholed walls. Not much color down here. And with a powerful pull Henry finds himself thrown into a room with air. It's a small room, but it has air and he can stand. Henry pulls off the mask and takes in a deep breath. He also takes off the tank and lays it on the ground beside him.

"This is it." Henry says out loud. "I've done it!:

Henry shines the light around to get a better look at his surroundings. It's like a cave. The walls are gray and dirty. The floor also seems to be made of rock. He clears out his nose of water and continues to observe the room. There was no way out. At least not for an air breather. Henry sits there a bit as if waiting for his invitation to a dinner party to arrive. He shines his flashlight back and forth every so often. Now and then he shines it back towards the hole he came in. Half expecting to see two eyes looking back at him. But after what feels like hours, Henry starts to wonder if they forgot about him in there? How could they? He didn't know how their customs. Maybe this was normal? Maybe they thought he just needed some rest as they prepared him to meet their ruler?

As Henry laid their shining his light back towards the hole he realized that the flashlights power was starting to fade. "No! No! No!" he gasped. "Oh c'mon! Not now!! Shit." Little by little the light started to fade and Henry kept shaking it more and more. Pounding the tiny flashlight against his hand is if that would somehow give it more power.

"No! No! No.. are you serious?"

The flashlight keeps failing. "Please, god. Please." Henry cried out in the darkness. Even if he had to swim out of the hole to escape, he would have no idea which way to swim. The water was so murky and dark that it would be impossible to find his way. And for that matter. Which way? In the dark you can hear Henry still trying to shake the flashlight to get it to work. Every third shake or so a tiny flash of dulled light comes out of the bulb dying bulb. Barely lighting the cave. With every other shake Henry swears he can see eyes on the surface of the water. "What do you want??!" He screams out into the black. He frantically shakes the flashlight more and more. And off and on he sees the more and more sets of eyes just skimming the surface. He keeps shaking and the little flashlight keeps rattling but this time there's no more juice. Henry starts to cry out. You can hear his panicked breathing and feet shuffling around on the rock floor. He thought, how did it come to this? Would the squid people bring him a new flashlight? Would they take him back up to the warehouse room with the pillars? Even if he makes it back to that room what next? Would the elevator come back down for him? You can hear Henry begin to shake from the cold and fear. His teeth are chattering and his breathing is getting tighter. Henry does his best to rub his arms back and forth to keep warm but it doesn't seem to help.

Henry yells out "HELLO!?"

Still no sounds in the darkness. Just his own voice bouncing back off the closed in walls.

"Lucy.." Henry says teeth chattering. "Lucy if you can hear me. Forgive me. I should have never left home."

Henry begins to calmly repeat "I wanna go home. I wanna go home. I wanna go home. I wanna go home. I wanna go home." It eventually turns into a raging yell. As if Henry is just fighting the fear and the cold. "I wanna go home!!! I wanna go home!!! I wanna go home!!! I wanna go home!!!" And still nothing but darkness and silence. Just his voice echoing off the cavern walls.

Suddenly Henry yells out "OWE!" You can hear panic set into his voice as he yells out again "OUCH! You fucker!!" Henry begins to scream uncontrollably as he flails around in his tiny cell. "NO!! NO!! NO!! NO!! AAAAAAAAAAA!!!" His body keeps smacking up against the cavern walls. "FUCK YOU!! OWE!!! NO!! NO!!!!! GET OF ME!!!!"

Henry's fighting for his life in the dark. Howls of pain! His screams of terror are only matched by the sounds of slithering. Relentless chewing and slurping. The sounds of bones cracking fill the small room. Flesh is being ripped and Henry's shouts quickly turn to silence. It only lasts a matter of minutes before the gnawing goes quiet. And the smacking sounds of tentacles overlapping each other. Small sounds of water rippling can be heard but otherwise, the dark eventually becomes deathly still.

Up above the in the city, it's raining tonight. New Yorkers are grilling. People are still excessively using their horns. Music is playing loud through an apartment window. Even higher above, the city lights sparkle in the rain. And nobody knows that under the surface of all that hustle and bustle, there's an entire world hidden away. Maybe on purpose. Maybe it's better that way. Safer for both species to avoid each other. Go our own ways and never seek each other out. Down alley ways and up through manhole covers. Are those screams? Can you hear them? Was Henry the only unlucky one tonight? How many more cracks and water ways are concealed in the basements of old buildings? Did you hear it? Was that a scream?

It's raining on a small house in Sheffield, Iowa tonight too. A little girl looks out her bedroom window and watches the rain. She also watches as a plane passes. It's so far in the sky that she can only see the flashing red lights. In a hurry she rushes to open her window and waves as hard as she can with a big smile. Her face lights up with the hope that her daddy is waving back. How many more planes will pass by through the years before Lucy realizes that her dad isn't coming back? Will she ever accept it?

Lucy is 32 years old now and has a family of her own. Even to this day when she sees a plane she looks up and waves. Not as enthusiastically as she did for many years as child. But it brings her peace now waving. And some days she gets butterflies in her stomach when she hears a car door shut in her driveway. She hopes that it's him. She hopes that he'll still look the same and that the years have been kind. Hoping that one day her daddy will walk into the room and tell her all about his adventures. Tell her all about the squid people.

The end.

Made in the USA
Columbia, SC
27 September 2018